The Witch in 204

Barbara Pease Weber

A SAMUEL FRENCH ACTING EDITION

FOUNDED 1830

SAMUELFRENCH.COM
SAMUELFRENCH-LONDON.CO.UK

FOR PRODUCTION ENQUIRIES

UNITED STATES AND CANADA
Info@SamuelFrench.com
1-866-598-8449

UNITED KINGDOM AND EUROPE
Plays@SamuelFrench-London.co.uk
020-7255-4302

Each title is subject to availability from Samuel French, depending upon country of performance. Please be aware that *THE WITCH IN 204* may not be licensed by Samuel French in your territory. Professional and amateur producers should contact the nearest Samuel French office or licensing partner to verify availability.

MUSIC USE NOTE

THE WITCH IN 204 was first produced at The Old Academy in Philadelphia, Pennsylvania in September 2011. The performance was directed by Christopher Wunder and the cast was as follows:

BELLA	Brianna June Tillo
SYLVIE	Marcy Hoffman
THELMA	Virginia Kaufmann
FANNIE	Lauri Jacobs
MABEL	Norma Kider
HERMAN	Steve Blumenthal
EVELYN	Loretta Lucy Miller
EUGENE	Nicholas Lutwyche

THE WITCH IN 204 was subsequently produced by the Truth or Consequences Community Theater in Truth or Consequences, New Mexico in September 2012. The performance was directed by Carol Anton and the cast was as follows:

BELLA	Lucille Benda
SYLVIE	Susie Wisdom
THELMA	Cathy Lacey
FANNIE	Ginger Henry
MABEL	Becky Burcher
HERMAN	Manion Long
EVELYN	Marie Bradley
EUGENE	Rick O'Neill

CHARACTERS

SETTING

An "Over-55" Condo Complex at the New Jersey Seashore

TIME

The Present

For John, Amy, and Ashley,
with loving memories of our time together at the New Jersey seashore.
xoxo
"The Witch in 204"

PREQUEL

(Curtain closed. Stage dark. Eerie organ/funeral music plays to a crescendo as an assortment of remote-controlled flameless candles are "lit" and a red spotlight slowly comes up on "BELLA's Den" in a wing downstage right in front of the closed curtain. BELLA's den is all black save for strategically placed nettings of cobwebs and a small table on which there is an assortment of prescription medication bottles and referenced paraphernalia. As the music fades, BELLA (a glamorous, sexy, seductive, exotic femme fatale with attributes of Bette Davis, Julie Newmar, Lauren Bacall, Kim Cattrall, Sharon Stone and Lady Gaga all rolled into one wickedly wonderful lady-killing/man-eating package) appears wearing a black negligee, feather boa and petit witch hat and sits at her table admiring her weapons of destruction. After the music stops, BELLA looks into the audience, regarding them as if they are her pupils and she a self-confident master instructor. BELLA then picks up her first of many prescription bottles, gives it an approving smile, and delivers directly to the audience with flair, determination and conviction, the following "poetic incantation" throughout which BELLA skillfully concocts her "witch's brew" by crushing tablets and emptying capsules from the assortment of prescription bottles into a golden chalice (filled with vinegar), the contents of which will fizz up and bubble over as BELLA delivers her final verse.)

BELLA.
Fluoxetine! Paroxetine! S.S.R.I.s!
Positively plausible alibis!
Why toil and trouble to *poison* an apple?
Simply sprinkle digitalis in a bottle of *Snapple!*
Prozac! Pristiq! Of course, penicillins!

Prescription pharmaceuticals – such *ideal* villains!
Wonderful witchcraft for *wickeds* like me,
Neurotin in a cup of tea?
No need to par boil an eye of newt!
Why fire up the caldron when Digoxin will suit?
An overdose you say?
Confirmed by the Laboratory!
But, she hid it *so* well!
Have fun in Purgatory!
Orgasmic – Oxycontin!
Oxycodone – *Exquisite!*
It's time to pay the pharmacy a visit.
Just a *few* Vicodin won't stir suspicion,
Substitution *not* permissible, says *this* physician!
Suicide? No!
Not her! Not ever!
Pour in some *Smirnoff.* Make it look even better!
Zoloft! Cymbalta! The depths of depression!
Toss yourself off a bridge! That'll teach him a lesson!
Fluoxetine, paroxetine, amoxicillin,
Prescription medications! Such *lovely* villains!
Pharmaceutical adjuvants to activate the hex,

(**BELLA** *delivers the next line directly to the audience.*)

Just wait and see what a scorned witch will do next!

(**BELLA** *pours the contents of a "special" prescription bottle (filled with baking soda) into the chalice filled with vinegar and as it bubbles over she throws her head back and emits a series of three a spine tingling cackles as the red spotlight fades to black and the remote controlled candles go dark. Eerie organ/funeral music resumes for a few seconds then fades as* **BELLA** *exits. It's now time to begin Act I and commence our journey to whack the witch.)*

ACT 1

Scene One

(Setting: Sylvia Goldberg's beachfront condo in Margate, New Jersey)

(At Rise: Early afternoon on the day of **SYLVIE** *and* **EUGENE**'s *wedding. Bridesmaids* **THELMA** *and* **FANNIE** *are assisting* **SYLVIE** *to get ready for the event.* **THELMA** *wears large thick-lens glasses as she is visually challenged.)*

THELMA. *(carrying in* **SYLVIE**'s *dress from the bedroom and carefully spreading it over a chair upstage left)* What a beautiful dress, Sylvie. You're sure to make a lovely bride.

FANNIE. I'm very honored you asked me to be one of your bridesmaids, Sylvie.

THELMA. So am I. I feel like a girl again!

SYLVIE. Who else would I ask? You are my dearest friends! And, of course, Mabel too.

THELMA. Wouldn't Mabel rather have been your Maid of Honor, Sylvie?

SYLVIE. Well, I did think about asking her. But, I think she's better suited for what she's going to do. Don't you?

THELMA. I see your point. After all those years of matchmaking, this will surely be Mabel's defining moment of glory.

FANNIE. But, Mabel didn't introduce Sylvie to Eugene. Sylvie met Eugene when she went over to Israel to see Barry and Rachel get married, remember?

THELMA. I sure do. Eugene seemed to have magically appeared just after Sylvie came back from Barry's wedding in Israel last year. In fact, he followed you home, didn't he Sylvie?

SYLVIE. Well, not exactly.

FANNIE. And, you two have been quite the couple ever since.

THELMA. It's such a shame that Barry can't make your wedding, Sylvie.

SYLVIE. I know. But it's more important that he stay at home with Rachel. You know, she's due any day now. And, then…can you believe it? I'll have my very first *great* grandchild!

FANNIE. Mazel Tov, Sylvie! How wonderful for you! *(She cries with a mixture of joy and sorrow or simply pure bipolarism, it's hard to tell.)*

THELMA. And, what a great excuse for another trip to Israel. With your *new* husband.

SYLVIE. Eugene and I are planning a trip to see the baby next summer. Or, maybe even this winter if I can't wait until then. Thelma, Mabel didn't tell you she was disappointed that I didn't ask her to be my Maid of Honor, did she?

THELMA. Are you kidding? For a yenta like Mabel, *this* is the absolute golden ring.

SYLVIE. I thought so too. That's why I asked her to officiate.

FANNIE. *(Tearing up)* On second thought, Sylvie, you may be sorry you asked me to be one of your bridesmaids. Seeing you and Eugene exchange vows, I'm sure to cry through the entire thing. I don't care if it is a just commitment ceremony instead of a real wedding. It's soooo romantic. *(**FANNIE** weeps tears of joy.)*

SYLVIE. *(handing **FANNIE** a tissue)* There, there now, dear. Here. Dry your eyes or you'll get all blotchy and everyone will think you've been eating clams again.

FANNIE. *(**FANNIE** takes tissue and dries her eyes.)* Thank you. Oh Sylvie, I'll miss you so much!

SYLVIE. Nonsense! Eugene and I will only be in Niagara Falls a week. Then we come right back home. No need for tears. *(SYLVIE hands FANNIE another tissue.)* Here. Blow.

FANNIE. *(FANNIE blows loudly.)* I can't help it. This is so romantic. Just like a Lifetime Television movie. *(FANNIE weeps again.)*

THELMA. Or, one of those Jasmine Johansson senior romance novels. *(THELMA proceeds as if telling a boy-meets-girl story.)* "Mysterious handsome gray haired stranger meets retired schoolteacher widow while she's out of the country attending her grandson's wedding in Israel."

FANNIE. *(helping THELMA along with the story)* "Then, the mysterious handsome gray haired stranger follows the old schoolteacher home to New Jersey."

THELMA. *(continuing with the tale)* "But, the schoolteacher widow doesn't want anything to do with the handsome gray haired mystery man so she hands him his walking papers."

FANNIE. *(finishing up the novetta)* "But, the magical mystery man refuses to leave her and after a summer filled with champagne and chaos, just as he is about to give up the quest to win over her affections and return to his native homeland, the old school marm realizes she can't live without the one person who…"

THELMA. *(continuing)* "…who, other than her dear departed husband, is likely to be the greatest love of her life and she begs him to stay with her in Margate, New Jersey and live…

FANNIE AND THELMA. …Happily Ever After!!!!

FANNIE. *(more boo hooing)* Oh, it's even better than a Jasmine Johansson senior romance novel. Sylvie's and Eugene's love story is sooo romantic. *(She sniffles and blows.)*

THELMA. Fannie, with all your crying I'd almost believe you were going through menopause. Except, you already did *that* 20 years ago. You *did* remember to take your pill today, didn't you?

FANNIE. *(Thinks)* Um. I forgot.

THELMA. I thought so.

SYLVIE. That explains it, dear. Hurry upstairs now and take your medicine so it'll kick in before the ceremony starts.

THELMA. Take two. I get the feeling you could use a double.

FANNIE. *(Exits to leave)* All right. But, don't start the ceremony without me.

SYLVIE. Of course we won't.

THELMA. *(After FANNIE exits)* Poor Fannie. She's been a mess ever since Herman's, you know...*mishap.* It *was* her idea, you know.

SYLVIE. Poor Herman. I didn't have the heart to ask Fannie if he's up to coming to the ceremony. She's so out of sorts as it is.

THELMA. *(laughing)* I think she feels guilty.

SYLVIE. I understand that. We Jewish women master the art of guilt. What I don't understand though is why they waited so long to get help.

THELMA. Herman was embarrassed to speak up. You know, Mabel being Herman's cousin and Fannie being one of Mabel's best friends and everything...

SYLVIE. But Mabel is the one who fixed them up to begin with. At last summer's Senior Social. They've been practically inseparable ever since.

THELMA. Mabel told me that Fannie and Herman spent that afternoon frolicking in the proverbial haystack. The entire afternoon! Who would have thought that old Herman had it in him?

SYLVIE. Well, Herman did used to be a Marine.

THELMA. That was 50 years ago!

SYLVIE. Then what happened?

THELMA. Well, they got carried away, I guess, and were running late to meet Mabel for dinner over in Atlantic City. By then, Herman suspected he had a bit of a problem but he tried to ignore it.

SYLVIE. Just like a man. Ignore a problem until it goes away.

THELMA. Not this time! Herman's problem kept getting growing and growing, if you get my drift. He told Fannie he didn't feel so hot and wanted to stay in for the evening.

SYLVIE. Then how did they wind up over at the casino?

THELMA. Well, Fannie tried to reach Mabel to tell her to take the jitney home. But Mabel had just won a penny jackpot and her machine was ringing and she didn't hear her cell phone.

SYLVIE. Mabel's always hitting on the pennies. She's so lucky!

THELMA. So, since Fannie doesn't drive at night, Herman ignored his *growing* concern and they went over to meet Mabel over at the Tropicana.

SYLVIE. Why does Fannie feel guilty?

THELMA. Fannie was the one who got Herman's prescription filled the day before. It was the first time Herman took the pills. He doesn't watch TV much so he didn't see the all commercials or know about "four hour" warning.

SYLVIE. I guess he knows now!

THELMA. I'd say he does! So, they get over to the Trop, look around for Mabel and don't you know, Herman puts five dollars into a Triple Lucky machine and doesn't *he* hit a jackpot!

SYLVIE. Why is it that everybody hits on the Triple Lucky except me?

THELMA. You have to play to win, Syl. Anyway, Herman got so excited about his jackpot he forgot that he was still *excited* about the "other thing."

SYLVIE. Oh my!

THELMA. By the time they finally caught up with Mabel at the buffet Herman discovered that he couldn't sit *down* to eat dinner because he was still so "*up*" if you get my drift.

SYLVIE. Oy!

THELMA. So, Herman tells Fannie and Fannie tells Mabel and Mabel asks the waitress to call for an ambulance because by this time Herman is in so much distress he can't walk to the parking lot to drive to the hospital.

SYLVIE. So, that's when the ambulance came?

THELMA. Yes! Then the paramedics put Herman on a stretcher and start to check him out and there's a crowd gathering around – everybody thinking he had a heart attack or stroke until one of the paramedics radios the hospital "We've got it under control, Charlie. Just another old geezer with a poker pecker from over doing it with the diddle drugs. Ten Four."

SYLVIE. What a shameful thing to say! I hope he was reprimanded!

THELMA. The crowd around them went wild! "Way to go, Pops – hope she was worth it." "How much do you charge, sailor?" That type of thing.

SYLVIE. How humiliating. Poor Herman.

THELMA. Herman vowed to never show his face in Atlantic City again.

SYLVIE. Well, that's probably a good thing. With him on a fixed income, I mean.

THELMA. Anyhow, that's why Fannie feels guilty. She's the one who got him the prescription.

(**FANNIE** *returns with* **HERMAN** *in tow.* **HERMAN** *is a bald mild manner gentleman of slight build.*)

FANNIE. I'm back.

SYLVIE. Just in time for a couple of pictures. Feeling better?

FANNIE. I guess so.

SYLVIE. That's good, dear. I was a little worried. Herman, it's so nice to see you up and about (**THELMA** *unsuccessfully stifles a chuckle and* **SYLVIE** *shoots her a look.*)... I mean, ah, how are your feeling?

HERMAN. I'm much better now. Thank you for asking. So, Sylvie! Today's your big day. Are you nervous?

SYLVIE. Yes, nervous and very excited. I almost feel like a school girl. I can't believe I'm really getting married again. Even if it is just a commitment ceremony. Would you mind doing the honors?

(She hands **HERMAN** *her camera and gathers* **THELMA** *and* **FANNIE** *for a group photo.)*

HERMAN. Eugene is one lucky son of a gun to land a gal like you, Sylvie.

FANNIE. Hey!

HERMAN. And, I'm a lucky duck myself to have you as my gal, Fannie.

FANNIE. That's more like it.

HERMAN. All right ladies, get ready. Say cheese on three. One. . Two…

(Before **HERMAN** *gets to "three"* **MABEL,** *dressed like a Rabbi, bursts in in a dither and out of breath not to mention extremely agitated. She ruins* **HERMAN** *'s shot and nearly knocks him over and causes him to drop the camera.)*

MABEL. Sylvie, Sylvie! Good! You're still here. I have to talk to you.

HERMAN. Hey! Take it easy, will you!

SYLVIE. For goodness sake, Mabel, where else would I be? I'm just about to go downstairs to the courtyard and get married.

MABEL. Sylvie! I have to talk to you *now! (She looks around at the others in the room.)* In private! I have *Information!*

SYLVIE. Mabel, all right! Calm down! What is it? What's wrong? Didn't the caterer show up?

HERMAN. They're here. Setting up. *(to* **FANNIE***)* You better get a move on before they run out of clams casino.

SYLVIE. Then what is it, Mabel? What's wrong?

MABEL. *(to* **FANNIE, THELMA** *and* **HERMAN***)* I need to speak with Sylvie alone. Go wait outside for a minute.

HERMAN. *(looking at his watch)* Is the Open Bar open yet?

MABEL. Herman, you shouldn't be drinking. That is, with your *problem* and all. Remember what the doctor said? Go on now. Go sit by the pool.

HERMAN. All right. C'mon Fannie.

THELMA. Oh no you don't, Mabel. We're staying right here. If you have "*Information*" you have to tell all of us at the same time. Those are *The Rules.*

FANNIE. Yes, Mabel! Those are *The Rules!*

MABEL. You and your *Rules!* This time it's different. This *Information* is just for Sylvie.

FANNIE. Herman, this is girl stuff. Go on down stairs. I'll meet you on the veranda. Save me a claims casino.

THELMA. Fannie, no clams! Remember your hives last time?

FANNIE. I forgot. *(beat)* Herman, save me a shrimp roll then.

HERMAN. Do you think it'll hurt if I have just one drink while I'm waiting?

FANNIE. No Herman! Remember what the doctor said. Have a V8 instead. Without the vodka.

HERMAN. Oh, all right. (**HERMAN** *exits.*)

THELMA. All right, Mabel. Enough is enough. Sylvie's getting married in ten minutes. What is going on?

SYLVIE. *(panic setting in)* It's Eugene, isn't it! Something happened to Eugene! Tell me, Mabel! Please! Is Eugene all right?

MABEL. Sylvie… I think you better sit down.

THELMA. Oh boy, here it comes. I knew Eugene was too good to be true. (**SYLVIE** *sits and* **THELMA** *and* **FANNIE** *gather around her.*)

MABEL. I was going over my notes for the ceremony. Thank you, by the way, for asking me to officiate. It's quite an honor for a yenta to play Rabbi for the Day.

SYLVIE. Mabel, please! What's happening?

MABEL. I was outside on the veranda, supervising the caterers and going over my notes for your ceremony. The h'ordeuvres *are* scrumptious by the way. Wait until you taste the salmon pate.

SYLVIE. Mabel!

MABEL. Okay, okay. So, there I was, on the veranda, minding my own business, and keeping an eye on Evelyn Greenbaum. Dressed to the nines she is and already knocking back vodka martinis like...

THELMA. Evelyn's back from rehab?

MABEL. Yes, yesterday. Not that it did her much good. She'll be completely schnockered in another 10 minutes.

SYLVIE. Mabel, get to the point, please.

MABEL. All right! So, there I am minding my own business...

THELMA. We know that! You're minding your own business. Then what?

MABEL. When out of the corner of my eye I see Eugene on the other side of the garden.

SYLVIE. He's all right then?

MABEL. Well, I didn't want to stare, but he was talking to the new neighbor.

FANNIE. We have a new neighbor?

MABEL. You know, the buxom red head* who moved into 204.

(Or, if more appropriate with respect to the actress playing **BELLA** *"blonde hottie", "ravishing brunette"...)*

FANNIE. Oh, right. I heard that someone finally bought old Mr. Silverstein's apartment. Oy, does that place need work. I haven't met her yet, though. Have you, Thelma?

THELMA. No, but Gloria Lichtenstein did. Yesterday. When she was coming back from the beach. Gloria said that the new neighbor must have had a *lot* of work done. You have to be AARP-eligible to buy in this building and Gloria said she didn't look a day over 30. Gloria said she had on big dark sunglasses, a black see though cover up which, apparently wasn't covering up very much. And neither was the skimpy black bikini she had on underneath.

SYLVIE. So Eugene was talking to the new neighbor. So what?

MABEL. Well, it looked to me like they were arguing.

SYLVIE. Arguing? About what?

MABEL. That's the thing, Sylvie. It sounded to me like they were having a lover's quarrel!

SYLVIE. Mabel, that's absurd. Eugene and I are to be married today. He doesn't have a lover.

FANNIE. Besides Sylvie, that is!

MABEL. Well, I heard Eugene say, "Bella, that was a long time ago. You must leave me alone once and for all. I have a new life now."

FANNIE. Her name is Bella?

THELMA. Maybe she's Eugene's ex-wife! Did Eugene tell you he had an ex-wife, Sylvie?

SYLVIE. No. Eugene has never been married.

THELMA. Ha! That's what you think! Maybe they never got divorced! Maybe Eugene is still married. You could be engaged to a *bigamist*, Sylvie!

SYLVIE. Mabel, if you were on the veranda, how could you have possibly heard them talking from across the garden? Did you have your hearing aid turned up to high?

MABEL. Um…well… I had a feeling that something wasn't kosher in the proverbial kitchen so I snuck around the side of the building to get closer so I could hear what was going on.

FANNIE. Shame on you Mabel! Don't you know that it's impolite to eavesdrop.

THELMA. Phooey. What else did you hear?

MABEL. Then, I heard Bella, the mystery woman, tell Eugene that if she couldn't have him then nobody else could either. That she knows all of his *secrets* and that if he gets married to another woman she'll…

FANNIE. Secrets? Sylvie, does Eugene have secrets?

THELMA. Fannie, have you ever known a man who doesn't have secrets?

FANNIE. Herman doesn't.

THELMA. That's right, Fannie. If you say so.

SYLVIE. She'll what, Mabel? What did she say she'll do?

MABEL. I'm not sure. Mr. Wiseman was coming off the beach with his German Shepherd just as the siren at the firehouse across the street went off. The dog started to howl… I think the siren hurt its ears…and I couldn't catch what else she said. It sounded like…it sounded like…

THELMA. Like what?

FANNIE. What did it sound like?

MABEL. Now, the dog was howling and the fire house siren was blaring…but…it sounded like…it sounded like she said that if Eugene got married to anybody but her she'd…

THELMA. What already?

MABEL. I know this is going to sound crazy.

THELMA/FANNIE/SYLVIE. WHAT DID SHE SAY???

MABEL. It sounded like she said she'd *"cast a spell and have a hex put on them."*

THELMA. A hex?

MABEL. Yes, a hex!

FANNIE. Put on who?

MABEL. On Eugene and Sylvie!

THELMA. Mabel, I think you're the one who's been knocking back the vodka martinis and not Evelyn Greenbaum. That's the craziest thing I've ever heard. Are you sure she said "hex?" She didn't say "sex?"

MABEL. Hmmm. Come to think of it, I guess she could have said "kiss and tell about the sex with them" not "cast a spell and put a hex on them." The damn dog was howling. I was trying to read lips.

THELMA. That explains it then. Our new neighbor must be a Call Girl. And Eugene must be one of her clients!

FANNIE. She must be blackmailing him. That must be "his secret" that she threatened to expose.

SYLVIE. I don't believe it! Eugene would never patronize a Call Girl!

THELMA. Wake up, Sylvie, and smell the pickled herring.

SYLVIE. No, not Eugene! It's not possible!

FANNIE. This is just our luck. We have a jealous psychotic prostitute for a new neighbor. As if there aren't enough dysfunctional people living in this building already.

MABEL. Then, she...she...

THELMA. She what?

MABEL. She kissed Eugene!

FANNIE. Where?

MABEL. Right, there! Right in the garden!

FANNIE. On the *lips???*

MABEL. Of course on the lips! She grabbed him by the lapels of his tuxedo and kissed him on the lips! Sylvie, by the way, Eugene looks so handsome today. Did he rent the tux from Steinman's?

THELMA. Did he kiss her back?

MABEL. Eugene told her to go back to her apartment. He promised to meet her there as soon as he told you the wedding was off. Sylvie, I'm so sorry.

SYLVIE. But Mabel, Eugene hasn't been here. He never came to tell me that the wedding is off.

(There is a knock at the door.)

MABEL. That must be him now. Right on time.

THELMA. Ho boy. This ought to be interesting.

SYLVIE. What am I going to do?

FANNIE. *(innocently)* Answer the door?

SYLVIE. I can't! This isn't happening! We're supposed to be getting married in five minutes!

THELMA. I'll answer it, then. *(**THELMA** opens the door. **HERMAN** enters carrying an envelope containing a note.)*

MABEL. Herman! Thank God! We thought you were Eugene.

FANNIE. Herman, what are you doing here? I told you I'd meet you downstairs.

HERMAN. I know, Fannie. But, I was at the bar... I was just going to have a V8, I swear...and Eugene came over asked me to give this to Sylvie.

(HERMAN hands SYLVIE a note in a sealed envelope.)

Here Sylvie. *(then to* **FANNIE***)* I'm going back down to the bar to watch the ball game until the wedding starts.

FANNIE. That's fine, Herman. I'll be down shortly.

SYLVIE. *(deflated* **SYLVIE** *reads the envelope)* To Sylvie Goldberg. Private and Confidential.

THELMA. Some Prince Charming he turned out to be. He dumps you on your wedding day for a jealous prostitute and he doesn't even have the manners to tell you in person.

FANNIE. Aren't you going to open it, Sylvie?

SYLVIE. I... I can't.

MABEL. *(eagerly)* Give it to me. I'll open it.

FANNIE. But the envelope says "private" and "confidential".

MABEL. I won't tell a soul. *(***MABEL** *takes the note from* **SYLVIE***.)* May I?

SYLVIE. Ah, I don't think... *(***SYLVIE** *takes note from* **MABEL***.)*

MABEL. *(cutting her off mid-sentence and snatching away the note from* **SYLVIE***)...*you don't think that you can read it. That's all right. I'll do it. *(She scans the note.)* Ha! I was right! So there, Thelma! My hearing's not so bad. I'm not so crazy after all now am I?

SYLVIE. What does it say, Mabel? Why did Eugene write me a note?

MABEL. Are you sure you want to hear this?

SYLVIE. Yes! No! I don't know! Just read it already.

MABEL. Okay. But, I think you better sit down first.

(She helps **SYLVIE** *to sit as* **THELMA** *and* **FANNIE** *sit or stand on both sides of* **SYLVIE** *and hold her hands as* **MABEL** *begins to read.)*

"My Dear Sylvie: I regret to inform you that I am not able to marry you today."

SYLVIE. That's it. Stop reading. I don't want to hear anymore.

MABEL. Wait. It gets better.

THELMA. How could it possibly get worse?

MABEL. *(continuing with the letter)* "The reason that I am unable to fulfill my commitment to you on what was to be the first day of the best of our lives…"

FANNIE. "The first day of the best of our lives!" That's so poetic. Eugene writes so eloquently, Sylvie!

MABEL AND THELMA. Fannie!/Shush!

FANNIE. Well, he does!

MABEL. May I finish?

FANNIE. What's stopping you?

MABEL. *(continuing)* "The reason that I am unable to fulfill my commitment to you on what was to be the first day of the best of our lives is entirely the fault of the new resident who inhabits the second floor dwelling formerly occupied by the Elder Silverstein who embarked on his journey to the great ever after when he slipped in the bathtub on the eve of the winter solstice."

FANNIE. *(crying again)* I don't care if he is an eloquent writer. This is terrible. He jilted you at the alter, Sylvie! And for a *younger* woman.

SYLVIE. *(handing FANNIE a tissue)* There, there now. The pills will kick in soon.

MABEL. Quiet, Fannie! If you stop interrupting I can get to the good part.

THELMA. Mabel, it's a "Dear Joan" letter. There is no good part.

MABEL. Quiet! *(continues reading:)* "Despite our best efforts to conceal my true identity throughout our courtship, I am saddened to say that a vile vixen with whom I was acquainted many moons ago has located my whereabouts and has come to capture my affections by any means possible, including through her evil wickedness."

SYLVIE. Mabel, that's enough. Please give me the note. *(She goes for the note.)*

MABEL. Wait, it's almost finished. I can't stop now.

THELMA. What does Eugene mean about concealing his true identity? Is he some sort of fugitive, Sylvie? Have you been helping to hide him from the mob?

SYLVIE. No! Of course not! I can't stand this anymore! Mabel, give me that note! *(She starts to chase* **MABEL** *around the room.)*

MABEL. *(evading her in chase)* Hold your horses, I'm almost finished. Then you can have it. *(continues reading)* "The reality is, Sylvie, that hell would surely freeze over before I would succumb to the imprudent folly of such a she-devil. It is because of this jealous sorceress I must leave you forthwith for your own safety as she has vowed to put a hex on me and on any other whose heart I hold dear but hers. I am, therefore, leaving town post haste for your safety and protection. I encourage you to do the same. Although your identity has not been revealed to her, dear Sylvie, out of an abundance of caution my love, I beseech you, please leave Margate, New Jersey at once. And, above all else, *Beware of The Witch in 204.* Lovingly yours, Eugene.

MABEL, FANNIE, THELMA AND SYLVIE. *The Witch in 204????*

(As the lights dim and the curtain closes we hear **BELLA** *off stage bellowing another blood curdling cackle.)*

(Blackout/Curtain)

Scene Two

(Setting: Same, about a half hour later.)

*(At Rise: **SYLVIE** is on the phone attempting to make an airline reservation. **THELMA** and **FANNIE** are with her.)*

SYLVIE. *(Pacing and frustrated on the telephone)* No, I don't have a computer. Because, I don't feel as though I need a computer. Well, I've managed just fine all these years without a computer, so... Yes, I know it's *possible* to make a reservation on line, *if* you have a computer, which I *don't*. I see. Then why did you ask for my credit card number? I don't understand. Why can't I just tell you where I want to go and you make the reservation for me on *your* computer? Isn't that what you're there for? I want to make a reservation to fly to Tel Aviv. ISRAEL. As soon as possible. Yes, I'll hold. *(to **FANNIE** and **THELMA**)* Whatever happened to customer service? These days you need an advanced degree in computer science just to make a flight reservation. *(back to phone)* Hello? Yes, I'm here. That's right, American Express. But I just gave you my account number and expiration date. You need it again? Well, you'll have to hold on a minute. I put it away. I have to go get it out of my wallet. Again! *(She exits with cordless phone to the bedroom.)* Unbelievable!

FANNIE. Oh, the poor thing! Getting stood up on her wedding day.

THELMA. Same thing happened at my wedding.

FANNIE. With Oscar?

THELMA. No, Harold. My first husband.

FANNIE. He got cold feet? He stood you up?

THELMA. No, I stood him up.

FANNIE. You didn't!

THELMA. Oh, it was just for a few hours. I was a young bride, I got nervous. I went to the hairdressers that morning and locked myself in the storage room.

FANNIE. How long were you in there?

THELMA. Long enough to go from a brunette to a red head. I thought I could disguise myself then sneak out the back door when nobody was looking.

FANNIE. What happened?

THELMA. It was a small room and the fumes from the hair color were making me nauseous. When I opened the door to try to make a run for it, there stood my mother, hand on one hip, the receipts for the wedding with the other. And, what a scowl she had on her face! (**THELMA** *imitates.*)

FANNIE. She made you go through with it?

THELMA. She told me that if I didn't I'd have to pay back my father for everything he spent on the big event. That made me even more nauseous so I figured that marrying Harold was the lesser of two evils.

FANNIE. Was Harold angry with you for making him wait?

THELMA. No. *(beat)* But I'll never forget the look on Harold's face when I walked down the aisle with a head full of flaming red hair! I looked like a cross between Lucille Ball and a Barnum & Bailey circus clown.

FANNIE. How long were you married to Harold?

THELMA. Twenty six wonderful years. When Harold passed, I thought my life was over.

FANNIE. But a few years later, you married Oscar!

THELMA. Yeah. *(beat)* Now I *know* my life is over!

FANNIE. Oh come on. Oscar's a great fellow.

THELMA. Yes, he is. I've been twice blessed to be able to share my life with good and honorable men. *(They sigh, then:)*

THELMA/FANNIE. Poor Sylvie!

THELMA. Well, on the bright side, she'll be there with Barry and Rachel for the birth of her first great grandbaby. That's got to cheer her up.

(**MABEL** *enters carrying a covered tray of hors d'oeuvres.*)

MABEL. Oy Vey!

THELMA. Is everyone gone? What did you tell them?

FANNIE. *(eyeing the hors d'oeuvres)* Oh, good, you salvaged some snacks. I'm starving!

MABEL. *(hands tray to FANNIE)* Help yourself. Where's Sylvie?

THELMA. Trying to make an airline reservation.

MABEL. Without a computer?

FANNIE. *(mouth full)* Yeah, and that's not so easy these days.

MABEL. I think we all ought to take a computer class over at the senior center. I'm going to sign us up.

THELMA. What would you use a computer for, Mabel?

MABEL. Well, for one thing, all these new fangled internet dating services you hear about have put good old fashioned yentas like me practically out of business. I think I may want to learn how to use a computer just to I can at least keep tabs on my competition. Maybe even start my own business. Yentas.R.Us.Dot.Com!

FANNIE. Good idea.

(SYLVIE enters from bedroom.)

SYLVIE. That's done. There's a flight leaving out of Philly at 9:30.

MABEL. Tonight?

SYLVIE. Yes, I'm sure I can make it.

THELMA. *(looking at her watch)* It won't be dark for a while yet. I'll drive you to the Greyhound Station in Atlantic City. You can get a bus right to the airport.

(FANNIE and MABEL look at each other as they both know that THELMA has a reputation of having less than a stellar driving record.)

SYLVIE. Oh, thank you anyway, Thelma. I don't want to trouble you. I just called for a taxi.

THELMA. No, I insist. Let me drive you. I'll be careful, I promise!

SYLVIE. *(looking worried as SYLVIE also knows THELMA's driving record)* Uh, well, all right then, I think I'm ready.

FANNIE. You go on ahead. I'll straighten up here and put everything away. I'll water your plants while you're gone Sylvie.

MABEL. And, I'll check your mail.

SYLVIE. *(starting to tear up)* Oh, you are all such wonderful friends. What did I ever do to deserve you?

MABEL. There, there now. It'll all be fine. While you're gone we'll get to the bottom of all this.

THELMA. I'm glad Eugene showed his true colors, Sylvie, before you, you know, married him. Even if it was just a commitment ceremony.

SYLVIE. Oh, Thelma, I can't explain it, but even though I'm not entirely sure about what is going on – one thing I do know is that Eugene loves me.

MABEL. *(rolling her eyes away from* **SYLVIE** *and trying to sound convincing)* Of course he does, dear.

SYLVIE. After what has happened today, you may not want to believe it, Mabel, but I know it's true. Eugene is upstanding and honest, to a fault. He wouldn't tell me he loved me if he didn't mean it.

FANNIE. What do you think he means, Sylvie? About *The Witch in 204?*

SYLVIE. I have absolutely no idea, Fannie. But, what I do know is that I've got to get going if I'm going to make that 9:30 flight. I've got to get away from here.

THELMA. You mean, because of Eugene's warning to escape *The Witch?*

SYLVIE. Truth be told, I want to escape the *neighbors.* I don't want to go to the grocery store and have people looking and me and whispering behind my back "Poor old Sylvie. Jilted at the altar." I'm stick to my stomach when I think about running into Evelyn Greenbaum and Gloria Lichtenstein who have no doubt by now voted me as the new President of their "Woeful Women's Club." I'm embarrassed enough already. I don't need to be pitied on top of it.

FANNIE. After all, Thelma, you know the new woman in 204 is not a "real witch". I'm sure that Eugene just referred to her as a *witch* because he's a gentleman and didn't want to use the "B-Word."

THELMA. Well then, shall we go?

MABEL. Okay, let's get out of here.

THELMA. You're coming too?

MABEL. Thelma, no offense, but I better come along to make sure you stay on the right side of the road. Remember what happened last time you drove to the bus station?

THELMA. *(sheepishly)* I know.

FANNIE. What happened?

MABEL. She shot out of the bus lot, careened over the center barrier, and clipped the rear end of a greyhound.

FANNIE. You hit a bus?

THELMA. Uh...no. No.

FANNIE. Then... Thelma! Not again!

THELMA. I barely grazed its tail. It wasn't even hurt *(beat)* that much. It got up and ran away.

MABEL. Right into the lobby of Trump Plaza!

THELMA. It was dark outside. I stopped driving at night right after that.

MABEL. Not right after. Remember what happened to Rhoda Bennett's pussy cat?

THELMA. Rhoda hasn't spoken to me since.

SYLVIE. *(rolling her suitcase)* Good bye, Fannie. *(She hugs* **FANNIE** *and kisses her cheek.)* Will you do me a favor?

FANNIE. Of course, Sylvie, what do you need?

SYLVIE. If Eugene should come back while I'm away, please be sure to give him this. It's very private so please take good care of it for me. *(She hands* **FANNIE** *an envelope addressed to* **EUGENE** *containing a note.)*

FANNIE. I will, Sylvie. You can count on me.

MABEL. Let's go. Before the sun starts to go down. I want to get back before the animal rights activists know that Thelma's behind is behind the wheel again.

(*SYLVIE*, **MABEL** *and* **THELMA** *leave together. As* **THELMA** *exist, she bumps into the door on the way out.* **FANNIE** *is now alone in* **SYLVIE**'s *apartment and continues to tidy up. She places* **SYLVIE**'s *note to* **EUGENE** *on the table next to the sofa. A few moments later, there is a knock on the door. An extremely inebriated and disheveled* **EVELYN GREENBAUM** *enters carrying a clutch purse and wearing an expensive suit with the shirt half untucked and pill-box hat askew on her head.*)

FANNIE. *(opening door thinking it is* **SYLVIE**, **MABEL** *or* **FANNIE**) What did you forget? Evelyn! What are you doing here?

EVELYN. *(Brimming with martinis and melodrama)* Sylvia! Where is Sylvia? Poor Sylvia! Poor, poor pitiful Sylvia. Where is she? *(looks around)* Where is she? *(calls out)* Sylvia! Sylvia! It's me, dear, Evelyn! Evelyn Greenbaum! Your soul sister in sympathy and solace. *(calling)* Sylvia! *(horrified to* **FANNIE**) Did she try to *kill* herself? *(calling out)* Don't do it Sylvia! Don't do it! Men are all pigs! All men are swine! It's not worth it! *They're* not worth it! *(bangs on bathroom door)* I should know! I married three of them. I gave birth to four of them. I took it on the chin when they dumped me for newer models. A worthless lot of selfish swine! All of them! Don't harm yourself, Sylvia. Be strong! Be brave! Have a heart of stone unbreakable in the face of heartbreak! You can do it, Sylvia! *(beat)* I'll give you the name of my therapist! He's expensive, but he's worth it.

FANNIE. *(under her breath)* He hasn't done you much good it seems.

EVELYN. *(spins around holding her head so it doesn't spin off)* *What* did you say?

FANNIE. I said, settle down, Evelyn. You're coming apart at the seams!

EVELYN. *(turning back to bathroom door)* Don't do it Sylvia! Just remember, men have no brains! Men have no heart! Men only have one organ! They think and feel with their...

FANNIE. *(shocked)* Evelyn!

EVELYN. What?

FANNIE. Sit down. Come sit down. I'll get you a cup of coffee.

EVELYN. Sylvia! I must speak with Sylvia! I know what's she's going though! I can help her.

FANNIE. *(under her breath)* I seriously doubt it!

EVELYN. *What* did you say?

FANNIE. *(getting the coffee)* I said, no doubt about it, Evelyn. I'm sure you can. But, I'm afraid, Sylvie's not here anymore.

EVELYN. *(misinterpreting* **FANNIE***'s meaning with even more martini melodrama)* Not here??? Oh no! She didn't... she's not... Oh no! Oh my! I'm too late! I'm *too* late. Poor, Sylvia! Poor, poor, poor, pitiful Sylvia. Tell me! How did she do it? Knife? Gun? Pills? Rope? How? Tell me? How? I've tried myself a time or two but I'm nothing but a coward. I've never had the courage to go through with it! Brave, brave, brave Sylvia! How did she do it? What method? I must know. Did she leave a note? *(She sees* **FANNIE** *crossing from kitchen to bathroom holding a bucket and mop and gasps in horror pointing with one hand while clutching her chest with the other.)* Did she leave a *mess*?

*(***FANNIE*** puts bucket/mop down and hands a cup of coffee to* **EVELYN** *but* **EVELYN** *does not drink it yet.)*

FANNIE. Evelyn! Get a hold of yourself. Sylvie's fine. She just left for the bus station in Atlantic City.

EVELYN. *(sits on sofa)* The bus station? *(thinks)* A bus! Brilliant! I should have thought of that! She's going to throw herself in front of a Casino Charter! Quick! Painless! Efficient! And, if she's successful and makes it look like an accident, it's the perfect way for her heirs to achieve a structured settlement from the bus company's liability carrier. She's always been so industrious. *(with arm in air, making a fist to recognize and honor the accomplishment and speaking to the heavens)* Kudos to you, Sylvie! I admire your spunk and can-do attitude.

FANNIE. Evelyn! Sylvie is *taking the bus* to the Philadelphia airport.

EVELYN. The airport? What on earth for? She *can't* jump out of an airplane. They lock the doors before takeoff.

FANNIE. Sylvie's on a 9:30 flight to Israel. She's going to be with Barry and Rachel for the birth of her first great grandchild.

EVELYN. Ha! That's what you think! I *know*! I *know*! You'll see her on the eleven o'clock news! "Retired New Jersey Schoolteacher Takes Nose Dive Off Control Tower at Philly International – News at eleven." Mark my words! *(holds her head)* Ohhh. I don't feel so good. Can you get me a couple of aspirin?

FANNIE. I'll check. *(She goes into **SYLVIE**'s bathroom and comes out.)* Sylvie must have packed it. I'll go get some from my place. Are you going to be all right here for a minute?

EVELYN. Hurry, oh, please hurry. My head is going to split in half.

FANNIE. I'll be right back. Drink your coffee. And, try not to throw up on Sylvie's sofa. All right?

EVELYN. All right. Just be quick.

*(**FANNIE** exits leaving the apartment door ajar.)*

EVELYN. *(sips her coffee)* Yeech! How can anyone drink black coffee? *(She takes flask out of her clutch purse, tops off the cup and sips. She puts the flask on the coffee table.)* Ahhh. Much better. *(She gets up and walks around **SYLVIE**'s apartment looking at framed photographs. She picks up a framed photo of **SYLVIE** and **EUGENE** and speaks to it.)* Sylvia, Sylvia, Sylvia. You poor old fool. Didn't I warn you? Didn't I tell you that if Eugene seemed too good to be true, he probably was? I mean, *really*, Sylvia, what could *you* possibly have to offer a man like Eugene at *your* age? I *heard* the rumors. They're no doubt all over Margate by now. A *younger* woman. A *rich* younger woman. A *mysterious*, rich younger woman. That's what he wants, Sylvia. Ha! That's what they *all* want. I should know! Don't say I didn't warn you. *(She sees the envelope addressed to* **EUGENE** *on the coffee table.)* Aha! I was right. She did leave a note! *(reads envelope)* "Private and Confidential – To Eugene from Sylvie." *(thinks)* Hmmm. Well, dear, Eugene's not coming back and my guess is that neither are you so why leave a perfectly good suicide note to waste?

(She opens the envelope and starts to read. As she does, **BELLA** *enters and stands at the doorway. She listens as* **EVELYN** *reads* **SYLVIE**'s *note out loud and, therefore, mistakes* **EVELYN** *for* **SYLVIE**.*)*

EVELYN. *(reads note)* "My darling Eugene, Everyone around here seems to think that I should be upset, angry and even suicidal because you unexpectedly postponed our wedding day. Rest assured that although I am disappointed, I still love you. Even though I'm not at all certain about what is going on I am quite concerned about you and the situation involving the new resident in 204. Why did you refer to her as "The Witch?" Is she *really* a *witch?* An evil one? If so, Eugene, I'm frightened for both of us. Isn't life ironic? Just when I finally got used to *your* being "otherworldly" a witch shows up on my doorstep and whisks you away from me. I'm following your advice to "beware" of her and have decided to visit Barry and Rachel in Israel to be there for my great grandchild's birth. Should you return before I do, you know where to reach me. Until we meet again, my precious genie – *(***EVELYN** *looks up quizzically, then to herself/audience.)* GENIE??? – you will forever be in my heart. Always, Sylvie."

BELLA. *(enters mockingly clapping dressed in a tight black skirt, black blouse, colorful/stylish shawl*, black stilettos and looking like a ravishing diva and speaks melodramatically and condescendingly.)* Brav-O. Bra-VO!. Isn't that sweet? A *love* letter. From a washed up old hag to a geriatric genie.

*(***EVELYN*** spins around, drops the note and holds her head with both hands.)*

EVELYN. Oh! You startled me.

BELLA. *(picking up the letter)* Sorry.

EVELYN. What do you want?

BELLA. Why, I've come to see *you*, of course. I see that you've been drowning your sorrows. *(She takes the flask that* **EVELYN** *left on the coffee table.)* May I?

EVELYN. Help yourself. Not much left though.

BELLA. Thank you. *(goes into the kitchen, pours coffee into a cup and tops it off from the flask, sips)* Ahhh. *Very* good.

EVELYN. To the last drop.

BELLA. You're not at all what I expected, you know.

EVELYN. I'm not?

BELLA. *(studying* **EVELYN***)* No. Not at all.

EVELYN. What did you expect?

BELLA. Oh, I don't know. More of a fighter, I guess. I thought I'd have my work cut out for me. But, looking at you, I can see I really overestimated. This won't be nearly as a difficult as I anticipated.

EVELYN. Who did you say you are? One of the wedding guests?

BELLA. That's right. I am the uninvited guest. Every wedding's gotta have at least one, to make things interesting, don'tcha think?

EVELYN. Look, I hate to be rude, but I've got a headache the size of Gibraltar and I really must be going.

---

* shawl must have a pocket sewn on the inside so as to conceal a small flask or small liquor bottle full of her special brew

BELLA. Plane to catch?

EVELYN. What? *(sees* **BELLA** *holding the note)* No, no. I think you must be confused…

BELLA. No! *You* are the one who is clearly confused! How desperate he must have been all these years waiting for me to have scraped the bottom of the wine barrel for a wretched lush like you!

EVELYN. I beg your pardon! There's no need for name calling. Now, if you don't mind, I'd like to be alone for a while. Since the wedding is off, it's probably best that you leave.

BELLA. Leave? Surely you must know by now, I *LIVE* here!

EVELYN. Here? In…

BELLA. This *building.* 204.

EVELYN. You? You're the *bitch* in 204?

BELLA. Now who's calling who names? No, *not* the bitch in 204. The *Witch* in 204!

EVELYN. *(shrugs)* Same difference.

BELLA. Ha! Not by a long shot! I don't hooooowwwwllll at the moon! But, girlfriend, have *you* looked in the mirror lately? *(She spins* **EVELYN** *around to face the mirror.)*

EVELYN. *(horrified by her slovenly image, covering her face with her hands)* Leave me alone! You *are* a witch! What did I ever do to you?

BELLA. You stole him from me, and I'm here to get him back.

EVELYN. I haven't stolen anything from you. I don't even know you!

BELLA. Don't play coy with me. Where is he?

EVELYN. Who?

BELLA. Genesis Elijia Nefarius Ivan Ethiopia the Twelfth!

EVELYN. *Who?*

BELLA. You've known him *how* long and you remain unfamiliar with his proper name? You need me to shorten it for you ? G.E.N.I.E!

EVELYN. G.E.N.I.E.? *Genie?* You mean, *Eugene?*

BELLA. How utterly common. A nickname. Disgusting!

EVELYN. Listen to me! I'm trying to tell you that I'm *not...*

BELLA. *(cutting her off)... Right* for Eugene. Yes, I am certainly aware of that. And, as Cleopatra as my witness, *Genesis Elijia* will soon be mine once again.

EVELYN. *(lying on couch)* Ohhhh. My head. I must be having an alcohol induced nightmare.

BELLA. Yes, I'd have to agree that your nightmare is just beginning.

EVELYN. When will I learn not to drink vodka martinis, gin and tonics and scotch sours in the same afternoon?

BELLA. Now *that's* a witch's brew if I do say so myself.

EVELYN. If I close my eyes and count to ten will you go away?

BELLA. Not a chance.

EVELYN. This worked once before. *(she puts her hands over her eyes)* Oh, the room is spinning, I have to do this quick. One, two, three, four...

BELLA. Look at me! I'm not finished with you just yet!

EVELYN. Go away! Five, six, seven eight...

BELLA. I said, LOOK AT ME! *(She takes* **EVELYN**'s *flask and empties it on top of* **EVELYN**'s *head.)*

EVELYN. Hey! I was going to finish that!

BELLA. Where is he?

EVELYN. He who? Eugene?

BELLA. If you *must!* Yes, "Eugene".

EVELYN. I have no idea!

BELLA. I don't believe you!

EVELYN. Isn't he with you?

BELLA. He *should* be. He *will* be!

EVELYN. Then leave me out of it. I'm just an innocent bystander.

BELLA. Innocent, my foot! You stole him from me! *(looks around)* He must be here somewhere. I'll find him!

EVELYN. Suit yourself. I have to sleep this off. I'm going bed. *(*EVELYN *begins to get up and* BELLA *pushes her back down.)*

BELLA. *(Angrily)* You are doing no such thing! *(*BELLA *thinks for a moment then changes her tone to fake friendly.)* That is, I mean, I think we should try to be *friends*, don't you? After all, I *am* the new kid on the block…so to speak. Why don't we try to forgive and forget?

EVELYN. Forgive and forget what?

BELLA. Our *differences*, of course. If I have in any way offended you just now, I deeply apologize. I have a wonderful idea! Let's drink a toast to our new friendship.

EVELYN. *(holding her head)* Uh, I think I've had enough for one afternoon.

BELLA. Nonsense! What's one trifle indulgence to celebrate our new friendship? In fact, I have just the thing! I just know you're going to *love* this! *(*BELLA *pulls out her own flask out from the hidden pocket in her shawl.)*

EVELYN. Nice shawl! Love the hidden pocket. May I ask where you got it?

BELLA. The Rack at Nordstrom! Where else? *(*BELLA *pours the "brew" into their coffee cups.)* Since we're best friends now, you can borrow it any time you like.

EVELYN. Why, thank you, uh… I just realized, I don't even know your name.

BELLA. Why, it's Jezebella, girlfriend. But, Genesis Elijia calls me Bella. *(*BELLA *raises her glass.)*

EVELYN. *(cattily)* I thought you didn't like nicknames, "Bella".

BELLA. Bella is *not* a nickname. Only Genesis Elijia may call me Bella – as a term of endearment.

EVELYN. Well, bully for Genesis Elijia. *(She raises her cup.)*

BELLA. To new *friends*! Daisies Up! *(She raises her cup.)*

EVELYN. L'chaim! *(EVELYN takes a large swallow and reacts in a big way to the brew's potency both verbally and physically.)* WOOOOO HOOOOOOOOO!!!!!!! My! That's quite a potent potion you've got there! *(takes another sip)* Aaaahhhhhhhh! But, it goes down smooth the second time.

BELLA. As my dear departed Granny used to say, "It'll grow whiskers on your chin and shave them off at the same time." Here. Have some more. *(She tops off EVELYN's cup.)*

EVELYN. *(noticing that BELLA isn't drinking)* You're not having any?

BELLA. You seem to be enjoying it enough for the both of us.

EVELYN. I've never had anything like this before. Smooth, yet with a kick.

BELLA. *(Sexily)* Like karate.

EVELYN. What did you say it is?

BELLA. I didn't.

EVELYN. *(holds her cup out)* Just another small drop?

BELLA. *(pours generously)* Why not a big one? *(She cackles a phony laugh in which EVELYN joins her.)*

EVELYN. *(Smacking her lips up mouthing up and down)* Uh Oh. I think the kick caught up with me. I can't feel my lips. *(more lip smacking with exaggerated facial expressions)*

BELLA. Well, you weren't planning on puckering up with anyone just now, were you? Just *relax*. Go with it.

EVELYN. *(with mouth numb as if after Novocaine)* I can't feel my tongue. *(Her tongue darts in and out of her mouth. She's now drooling.)* Are my teeth still in my mouth? I can't feel my teeth! What happened to my teeth??? I have to look in the mirror. I think I may have swallowed them. *(She attempts to get up several times unsuccessfully.)* Hey! I'm stuck! I can't get up. What was in that drink? I can't feel my toes! I can't move my legs! Where are my feet?

BELLA. *(Angrily)* Shut up!

EVELYN. *(with numb mouth – feelings hurt)* That's not a nice thing to say to a new friend.

BELLA. Friend! Please! *Friends* don't go around stealing other people's lovers.

EVELYN. *(numb, drunk and incredulous)* You haven't lived in Margate very long, have you?

BELLA. *(begins to search* **SYLVIE***'s apartment)* Genesis Elijia! Where are you? *(sing song)* Come out, come out wherever you are! You can't hide from me forever, you know!

EVELYN. Help! I'm stuck! Fannie! Somebody! Help!

BELLA. *(going into* **SYLVIE***'s bedroom)*
Go ahead, let him hear what a pathetic whiner you really are. Genesis Elijia Nefarious Ivan Ethiopia, the Twelfth! Ready or not, here I come!

EVELYN. *(numb)* Help! Somebody! You really are a witch, aren't you?

BELLA. You mean you liked me better when I was just a figment of your alcohol induced imagination? My feelings are hurt.

EVELYN. *(numb)* Help! Anybody! Help!

BELLA. *(returns carrying an odd teapot/watering can object with a lid)* A-Ha! Look what I found! *Nobody puts Genesis in the corner.* You thought you could hide him from me on the shelf in your bedroom closet! I *know* where he lives! *(She speaks to the teapot while lovingly caressing it.)* It's all right now, darling. Everything will be all right. Come out my sweet. It's time that we begin our new life together!

EVELYN. *(numb)* Lady, all *I* do is drink at little too much. *You* talk to teapots!

BELLA. I've heard just about enough from you!

*(***BELLA*** puts down the teapot, takes the cup and places it against* **EVELYN***'s mouth and forces her to drink the remaining contents and, as if feeding a baby, provides*

*sound effects "Yummmm, Mmmmmm Mmmmm
Mummmm, That's a good girl".* **EVELYN** *becomes mute
– she cannot move or speak – only groan and grunt as
she is stricken with paralysis.)*

EVELYN. MGGRGRAH. WAAHRRMGH! PHAAFFTTTT!

BELLA. Much better! *You* were beginning to give *me* a
headache. *(patting teapot)* Well, Genesis Elijiah and I
must be running along now. I would say it's been a
pleasure to meet you, but I'd just be fibbing. No need
to get up! We'll show ourselves out! Oh, before I forget,
I'll take *that* and leave *this* for Eugene. *(She takes the note
that* **SYLVIE** *wrote to* **EUGENE** *and rips it up. Then she takes
out an envelope from her cape pocket and reads the envelope
of the switched note.)* "To Eugene, From Sylvia." This one
is much more interesting reading. Rest in Peace, Sylvia
Goldberg. It won't be long now. And, don't worry, I'll
take very good care of Genesis. He won't miss you one
bit! *(She exits cackling.)*

FANNIE. *(off stage cheerfully)* Hello. My, what a lovely wrap!
Neiman Marcus or Bergdorfs? I don't believe we've
met. I'm Sylvie's neighbor. Fannie Green. You must be
Sylvie's niece from Haddonfield.

BELLA. *(angrily, off stage)* Get out of my way!

FANNIE. *(hurt and offended)* Excuse me! I was just trying to
make polite conversation. Hey! What are you doing
with Sylvie's teapot! That's the souvenir she brought
home with her from her trip last summer. Give that
back!

BELLA. It's mine now. Move it grandma!

(There is a loud crash.)

FANNIE. Owww! You didn't have to knock me over! I could
have broken something. Didn't your mother teach you
any manners! Hey! Come back here! Give back that
teapot or I'll report you to building security! Hey!
Thief! Robber!

*(***FANNIE*** *hears* **EVELYN** *groaning in the apartment.)*

I'm coming, Evelyn, I'm coming! (*She enters the apartment limping from her fall.*) Hold your horses, Evelyn. I just got steamrolled out here by a teapot thief from Bergdorf's. (She enters the apartment.) What is that woman doing with Syvie's teapot? I'm calling Security. (*She picks up phone and looks around.*) Did she take anything else? Money? Jewelry? Why didn't you stop her?

EVELYN. *(Novocaine mouth)* AAAGGHHH!!! EELPH EEEE!!!!!

(*Translation: "Aaagghhh! Help me!"*)

(**FANNIE** *sees* **EVELYN** *frozen on the sofa. She hangs up and rushes to* **EVELYN**'s *side.*)

FANNIE. Evelyn! Evelyn! What happened? What's the matter?

EVELYN. *(Novocaine mouth)* HEE IG IS OU EE. ELK EE. AAAGGHH!

(*Translation: "She did this to me. Help me! Aaagghhh!"*)

FANNIE. Evelyn, I can't understand you! *(touches* **EVELYN***)* You're so cold! And, hard as a rock! Who was that woman? Did she do something to you?

EVELYN. *(Novocaine mouth)* Ex!. Curr ghe rorice!

(*Translation: "Yes! Call the police!"*)

(*We hear* **MABEL** *and* **THELMA** *offstage in a heated dispute about the color of a traffic light and continue to argue as they enter.*)

THELMA. I'm telling you, the light was still green!

MABEL. It was yellow!

THELMA. Green!

MABEL. Yellow! It changed color right before you went through it.

THELMA. It did not. I was half way across before it turned.

MABEL. Yes! *Red!*

THELMA. It's not my fault! Quit blaming me. The thing should have been on a leash. The policeman even said so.

MABEL. Then why did he give you a ticket?

THELMA. If you think I'm so terrible behind the wheel then why don't *you* get *your* license renewed and *you* drive next time?

MABEL. Maybe I will. For the sake of all of the family pets in South Jersey! *(She sees* **FANNIE** *hovering over* **EVELYN** *on sofa.)*

THELMA. *(to* **FANNIE***)* What's *she* doing here?

EVELYN *(Novocaine mouth)* WELF EEEEE REEEESSEEEEEE! EEEE REEEEDE HALPH! CULL UN URULEMSA.
(Translation: "Help me, please! I need help! Call an ambulance!")

THELMA. What did she say?

EVELYN. *(Novocaine mouth)* WELF EEEEE! CRULL YME UN UN' REEEESSEEEEEE!
(Translation: "Help me! Call nine one one! Please!")

MABEL. *(with mock sarcasm/ concern)* Evelyn, you *haven't* been *drinking,* have you?

EVELYN. *(Novocaine mouth)* REEEESSEEEEEE! CUUULL WYNE UN UN. WY EEEET UN UNUNUNCE.
(Translation: "Please! Call nine one one. I need an ambulance!")

MABEL. Just a rhetorical question.

EVELYN. AAAGGGHHHH!
(Translation: "Aaaggghhh!")

THELMA. Come on, Evelyn, I'll walk you upstairs so you can sleep it off.

EVELYN. EEEEEEEEEEEEEEEEEEEEE!!!!!

THELMA. *(struggling to get* **EVELYN** *up)* Come on. You can do it. *(She tries unsuccessfully a few times but only manages to lift* **EVELYN** *slightly off of the sofa. Each time* **EVELYN** *falls backward on sofa still in her frozen position.)* Evelyn! I can't do this by myself. You have to cooperate.

EVELYN. *(Novocaine mouth)* CULL DA RORICE! MELPH
EEEEEE!
(Translation: "Call the police! Help me!")

MABEL. What did she say?

FANNIE. I can't understand a word! Feel her arm. It's like
rigor mortis!

THELMA. Ewwwwwwww! *(Having just touched* **EVELYN,**
THELMA *wipes her hand on* **MABEL.***)*

FANNIE. I don't know what happened to her. She was
coherent before I left but she's been this way ever
since I got back.

MABEL. Back? From where?

FANNIE. I went up to my apartment to get her some aspirin.
She came here looking for Sylvie and then started
complaining she had a headache.

THELMA. Headache. Speech impairment. Rigidity. Those
may be signs of a stroke!

MABEL. Was she walking crooked?

FANNIE. *(matter of factly)* No more than usual.

MABEL. We better call an ambulance!

(**MABEL** *rushes to phone and calls 911.*)

EVELYN. *(Novocaine mouth)* RHYNELLY! CULL IYM RUN
RUN!
(Translation: "Finally! Call Nine One One!")

MABEL. *(phone conversation fades as she walks with phone into
kitchen area)* Hello, we need an ambulance at Jerome
Gardens in Margate. Apartment 302. Come quickly.
I'm not exactly sure. My neighbor may have had a
stroke. She's talking funny and she was complaining of
a headache and she's very stiff...

THELMA. *(to* **FANNIE***)* Did she pass out? Did she throw up?

FANNIE. No! She other than complaining about a headache
and being tipsy of course, Evelyn seemed fine when I
left. She was a bit out of sorts what with the wedding
being called off – but out of sorts is typical for Evelyn.

EVELYN. *(Novocaine mouth)* DEINT AWK UBUT EEE EKE EEM UT ER.

(Translation: "Don't talk about me like I'm not here.")

FANNIE. I would have come back sooner but Gloria Lichtenstein nailed me getting off the elevator and she can talk the ears off a donkey. Then, some strange woman came barreling out of Sylvie's apartment, knocked me over and stole Sylvie's teapot!

MABEL. *(returning)* The ambulance will be here in a minute.

THELMA. A woman knocked you over and stole Sylvie's teapot?

MABEL. What are you talking about? Sylvie's teapot is right over there. On the stove.

FANNIE. Not *that* teapot. Remember that teapot Sylvie bought last summer when she went to see Barry and Rachel get married.

THELMA. Oh that. Didn't she buy it at an outdoor market when she went to Egypt for a few days before she came home?

MABEL. Who'd want to steal *that* ugly thing?

EVELYN. *(Novocaine mouth)* GHA RRRRREEECCCCCHHHA UGGNNNNN FOOOOO OHHHHHH FUUURRREEERRR

(Translation: "The Witch in 204!")

FANNIE. What, Evelyn? What are you trying to say?

EVELYN. *(Novocaine mouth)* GHA RRRRREEECCCCCHHHA UGGNNNNN FOOOOO OHHHHHH FUUURRREEERRR

(Translation: "The Witch in 204!")

MABEL. Evelyn, we can't understand you.

(**EUGENE** *enters followed by* **HERMAN.**)

EVELYN. *(Novocaine mouth)* GHA RRRRREEECCCCCHHHA UGGNNNNN FOOOOO OHHHHHH FUUURRREEERRR

(Translation: "The Witch in 204!")

EUGENE. She said, "*The Witch in 204.*"

FANNIE. Eugene! You came back!

EVELYN. *(EVELYN gives one final utterance then passes out.)*
AAAAGGGHHHHHHHH!

(BELLA bellows another off stage cackle as the lights fade to black.)

(Blackout/Curtain)

End of Act One

ACT TWO

Scene One

(Setting: The same, a short while later.)

(At Rise: The paramedics have taken **EVELYN** *. to the hospital.* **MABEL** *went with them.)*

(**FANNIE, EUGENE, HERMAN** *and* **THELMA** *are in* **SYLVIE** *'s apartment.* **HERMAN** *is hungrily partaking in the last of the hors d'oeuvres.)*

HERMAN. *(holding an hors d'oeurve on a toothpick)* Do you think Sylvie has any spicy brown mustard in her refrigerator?

FANNIE. Herman, how can you possibly eat after all that just happened?

HERMAN. I'm hypoglycemic. If I don't eat regularly I get...

EUGENE. Where is Sylvie? Please, Thelma. You must tell me.

THELMA. Now you just settle down, sailor. Sylvie's our dear friend and you really disappointed her today with your disappearing act. It's *our* turn to ask questions. Why did you go to all the trouble to plan a big wedding celebration only to leave Sylvie high and dry at the alter? And, what's all this monkey business about a witch in 204?

FANNIE. I'm *very* disappointed in you, Eugene. You're not the *man* I thought you were.

EUGENE. *(to himself, stage whisper)* If you only knew.

HERMAN. Is there any whitefish left?

THELMA. And, while we're at it, why weren't you and Sylvie going to have a *real* wedding? Why just a commitment ceremony? What are you trying to *hide?*

FANNIE. Yeah! What *are* you trying to hide? Have you got another *wife* tucked away on the side someplace out there?

EUGENE. No! Of course not!

HERMAN. *(holds up a mini hot dog on a toothpick)* Are these mini wienies kosher?

FANNIE. *(exasperated)* Herman! Yes! I think so.

HERMAN. Are you sure? Because if they're not then…

FANNIE. I don't know, Herman! Just eat it already. If lightning doesn't strike you dead then they must be kosher.

HERMAN. *(holds mini wienie under* **FANNIE***'s nose)* Does this smell kosher to you?

FANNIE. For goodness sake, Herman! If you're that concerned about it, don't eat it!

*(***HERMAN*** sniffs at it contemplates if it is kosher.)*

THELMA. Or, are you a fugitive from justice and afraid of being caught? Which is it?

EUGENE. Pardon my precarious perception, but it is apparent that the two of you watch entirely too much day time television. You should really spend the prime of your lives more wisely. Like volunteering to read for the blind, for instance, or…

THELMA. Oh *no you don't!* We're not the ones on trial here. You don't get to twist this around!

FANNIE. She's right! Which is it? Bigamist or fugitive? Confess!

HERMAN. *(deciding that the wienie is "safe", pops it into his mouth then howls loudly as if in terrible pain and having a heart attack)* OOOWWWWWWW!

(They all stop and look at **HERMAN***, horrified to think the wrath of God has fallen upon him for eating a non-Kosher wienie.)*

HERMAN. *(sheepishly, holding up a toothpick)* Forgot to take out the toothpick.

(Everyone shakes their head, rolls their eyes and continues with the conversation.)

EUGENE. The commitment ceremony was Sylvie's idea. I want her to be my wife, in any manner of her choosing. Where is she? Did Sylvie leave Margate?

FANNIE. Thelma drove her to the bus in Atlantic City.

THELMA. Well, almost. She had to take a taxi for the last few blocks because of the darn poodle.

EUGENE. Then, she's leaving town. Good. She read my note.

THELMA. Actually, Mabel read it. To all of us.

FANNIE. And, we have plenty of questions, buster!

HERMAN. *(holding a snack on a toothpick and talking with his mouth somewhat full)* Fannie, give the guy a break why don't you? It was his wedding too. Can't you see? He's just as torn up about this as everyone else is. *(picking up a near-empty soda bottle)* Is this the last of the diet Coke? *(He pours what's left into his glass.)*

FANNIE. I wouldn't have expected you to take his side, Herman. Does this mean you think it would be okay to leave me standing at the altar too?

HERMAN. *(stops eating)* Are you saying that you'll marry me?

FANNIE. I didn't hear a proposal.

HERMAN. I… I… *(clears throat and swallows)* Fannie, will you…

FANNIE. *(admonishing)* I don't see you on your knee.

HERMAN. *(He struggles to kneel but can't and shrugs.)* It's a replacement. It doesn't bend as well as the original.

FANNIE. Oh, well, okay then. You were saying?

HERMAN. Fannie, I've loved you from the moment I watched you belly dance at the senior social last year. Will you do me the great honor of becoming my wife?

FANNIE. Well… *(beat)*… Yes! But, I want a *real* wedding! Not a commitment ceremony.

HERMAN. You can have anything you want, Pumpkin! Just name it. *(to* **FANNIE**, *confidentially, stage whisper)* Let's, er..let's just skip packing the honeymoon helpers, shall we?

FANNIE. Yipee! I'm getting married! I'm getting married!

(She does a "happy dance" and plants a big kiss on **HERMAN**.*)*

THELMA. Congratulations, Fannie. We'll plan an engagement party for you a little later. *(pointing to* **EUGENE***)* I'm not quite finished with him yet.

EUGENE. Mabel should not have read the note. It was private. It was meant only for Sylvie. Where is she going? Please, you must tell me.

THELMA. Not that it's any of *your* business, you fugitive bigamist heartbreaker you, Sylvie is taking the bus to the Philadelphia airport. She's got a ticket on a 9:30 flight.

EUGENE. I am *not* a bigamist. Nor am I a fugitive. I will answer all your questions in due time. You have my word. First, tell me. Where is Sylvie traveling?

THELMA. That's all you're getting out of me. *(She tsks.)* You don't even deserve that much.

FANNIE. Oh! Here. I almost forgot! Sylvie said if you come back I should give you this. *(She hands* **EUGENE** *the note and he reads.)*

(The telephone rings. **THELMA** *answers.)*

THELMA. Hello. Mabel! *(They all gather around the* **THELMA**.*)* How is Evelyn? I see. What did the doctor say? Ugh! That's awful. Uh huh. Uh huh. Really! What a relief! Well, keep us posted. All right. Thanks. *(She hangs up.)*

HERMAN. How is she?

FANNIE. What did she say? What did she say?

THELMA. She's conscious. It wasn't a stroke, thank God. They suspect a combination of *Jack Daniel's* and some kind of pills. The Emergency Room doctor told Mabel it was a close call. He said that it was lucky that Evelyn's friends were here to call an ambulance right or else it could have been a real tragedy.

FANNIE. She'll be all right then? Thank goodness!

THELMA. Mabel said they'll probably want to keep her overnight for observation.

FANNIE. You know, I would have been glad to ride in the ambulance to the hospital with Evelyn. But, Mabel insisted that *she* go instead. Will you drive me over to visit her a little later, Herman? Then, maybe we can stop at Walgreen's on the way home so I can pick up this month's issue of *Modern Bride.*

HERMAN. Of course, Muffin. You know, I was surprised that Mabel wanted to ride in the ambulance with Evelyn. Mabel has always been squeamish about medical procedures. And, maybe I was wrong, but I had the impression that Mabel wasn't all that fond of Evelyn.

THELMA. Oh come on, Herman!

HERMAN. I'm sorry. That wasn't a nice thing to say at a time like this.

THELMA. No, I mean, wise up! You mean to tell me you don't know *why* Mabel wanted to go to the hospital with Evelyn?

FANNIE. Because she was concerned about her, of course.

THELMA. Fannie, how *long* have we known Mabel?

FANNIE. Ohhhhh! *(She laughs.)* In all the commotion, *that* didn't even cross my mind.

HERMAN. What?

THELMA. Herman, Mabel's your *cousin.* You've known her longer than any of us. You mean you really don't *know?*

HERMAN. Know what?

FANNIE. Men! Such innocent sheep!

THELMA. Let me spell it out for you. Who just called off his wedding?

HERMAN. *(points to* **EUGENE***)* Him.

THELMA. Besides Him!

HERMAN. Uhh. Who?

THELMA. Your great niece! Mabel's grand daughter, Bonnie. That's s who!

HERMAN. Oh. *(beat)* I see. *(He clearly doesn't.)*

THELMA. Bonnie broke off her engagement because her no-good corporate attorney fiancé was messing around with his lady lawyer boss to climb the corporate ladder quicker. Now, I ask you, what is the hospital *full* of?

HERMAN. Lawyers?

THELMA. Besides lawyers!

HERMAN. Sick people?

THELMA. Herman!

HERMAN. I don't know! Bedpans?

THELMA. Doctors!

HEMAN. Oh. *(beat)* I see. *(He's clueless.)*

FANNIE. Herman, what Thelma is trying to say is that Mabel, being the yenta that she is, wanted to use Evelyn as an excuse to hang around the hospital and scope out the young residents.

THELMA. Phooey on the residents. Mabel's camped out in the waiting room next to the surgical suite.

HERMAN. Evelyn's in surgery?

THELMA. No! She just had her stomach pumped in the Emergency Room.

HERMAN. Then why is Mabel…

FANNIE. Because having a husband who is a surgeon is a status symbol. Mabel could really wear her yenta crown with pride if she fixes up Bonnie with a surgeon.

HERMAN. Oh. I see. *(He doesn't get it.)*

EUGENE. *(holding note)* Sylvie didn't write this.

FANNIE. Yes she did.

EUGENE. No, she did not. Of this, I am certain.

FANNIE. Well, she didn't *type* it, that's for sure. She doesn't have a computer. You should have heard her on the phone trying to make an airline reservation.

EUGENE. She's flying somewhere? Where?

THELMA. Don't tell him.

FANNIE. Oh. Thelma, what does it matter now? *(to* EUGENE*)* Sylvie's going to stay with Barry and Rachel until after the baby comes.

EUGENE. Israel. Good. That should be far enough.

THELMA. Let me see the note. *(She takes note and holds it close to her face/glasses.)* This is not Sylvie's handwriting. It's too sloppy.

FANNIE. Let me read it. *(reads note)* This is a suicide note! Evelyn was *right.* Sylvie does plan to kill herself. *(looks more closely)*

THELMA. Don't be ridiculous. Sylvie isn't going to kill herself.. *(takes back note and holds it to her face)* This is a fake. *(reads again)* I'm confused though. Why does it say "Dear Genesis Elijia" and not "Dear Eugene"?

EUGENE. Fannie, where did you get this note?

FANNIE. *(distraught)* Sylvie *gave* it to me. How do you *know* she didn't write it? Do the rules of etiquette say that you have to use perfect penmanship when writing a suicide note?

THELMA. Fannie, Sylvie used to be *school teacher.* She *graded* her pupils on penmanship. Do you really think she'd leave behind a sloppy suicide note?

FANNIE. I guess not. Not when you put it that way.

EUGENE. *(to* FANNIE*)* When? When did Sylvie give you the note?

FANNIE. She handed it to me just before she left for the bus station. Sylvie told me if I saw you to give it to you. She must have had a feeling you'd come back.

EUGENE. She knows me very well. That's why I wanted her gone.

THELMA. What a mean thing to say!

EUGENE. I mean, that's why I wanted her to go away. Just for a little while. Until I get the affairs sorted out here.

FANNIE. So! You are having an affair!

EUGENE. Please be abundant with benefit of doubt. I intended the term to refer to business, not pleasure.

FANNIE. Oh.

THELMA. Fannie, why don't you and Herman go to the hospital and check on Evelyn and Mabel. If Evelyn is up to talking, maybe she can give us some clues.

EUGENE. *(to FANNIE)* Did you show the note to Evelyn when she was here?

FANNIE. No, but I put it right here, on the table, so you would see it if you came back. Evelyn may have seen it.

HEMAN. Do you think Evelyn somehow switched Sylvie's note with a different one?

EUGENE. I'm certain that the note Sylvie left for me was switched. But not by Evelyn.

HERMAN. Then who would have switched it?

EUGENE. Jezebella.

THELMA. Who? The *witch in 204?*

EUGENE. Yes. I'm certain it was she who conversed with Fannie.

FANNIE. That's what Evelyn was trying to tell us!

THELMA. Why would she switch the note... *(beat)*...unless...

FANNIE. Unless, she wanted you to *think* that Sylvie killed herself.

THELMA. Leaving the door open for her to swoop down like a chicken hawk and snap you up!

HERMAN. But, Sylvie wasn't even here at that point, was she Fannie?

FANNIE. No, Sylvie had already left when Evelyn came.

EUGENE. I'm both fearful and relieved as I believe I know what is likely to have happened.

THELMA/FANNIE/HERMAN. What?/What Happened?/Tell us.

EUGENE. I suspect that Jezebella must have mistaken Evelyn for Sylvie. After all, Evelyn was here in Sylvie's apartment.

FANNIE. I thought that the witch, I mean Jezebella, was one of Sylvie's nieces from Haddonfield at first.

THELMA. *(reading note again)* Then *you* must be Genesis Elijia?

EUGENE. My given name is Genenis Elijia Nefarious Ivan Ethiopia *(beat)* the Twelfth.

HERMAN. Now that's a tongue twister if I ever heard one. No wonder Sylvie calls you Eugene.

THELMA. But, the witch didn't know that. Which is why the note reads "Dear Genesis Elijia" instead of "Dear Eugene".

EUGENE. I'm afraid so.

FANNIE. Eugene, why do you call her a witch? Is Jezebella a real witch?

HERMAN. Fannie, there are no such things as ghosts, witches or UFOs. You've got to stop watching the SciFi channel.

(SYLVIE enters, pulling her suitcase on wheels behind her. She leaves the door ajar.)

SYLVIE. Eugene!

(EUGENE goes to SYLVIE, they embrace.)

EUGENE. Sylvia, please accept my sincere and heartfelt apology. I am deeply distressed that I disappointed you today in front of our friends. I do hope you will forgive me and that we can be married as soon as it is safe for us to exchange vows of commitment.

SYLVIE. Oh, Eugene, I knew...

THELMA. Quick! Shut the door! In case she comes back

(FANNIE runs to door, closes and locks it.)

SYLVIE. In case who comes back? The witch?

FANNIE. Yes! The witch in 204! She tried to kill Evelyn Greenbaum!

SYLVIE. *(horrified)* Kill Evelyn? When? Why?

EUGENE. She thought that Evelyn was you, Sylvie. And, as I feared, she attempted to kill her, thinking she was you.

FANNIE. She tried to poison her with a lethal potion of witches brew and *Jack Daniel's*.

SYLVIE. How horrible! How is Evelyn? Where is she?

THELMA. She had her stomach pumped over at Atlantic City Hospital. Mabel went with her. The doctor told Mabel she got there in time.

SYLVIE. Thank goodness!

HERMAN. Did you decide against visiting Barry and Rachel, Sylvie?

THELMA. Yeah! What are you doing here? It's not safe for you.

SYLVIE. Well, I was about to get on the bus and I got angry.

EUGENE. I understand, Sylvie. I'll go to my grave trying to make this up to you.

SYLVIE. No, no. Not angry with you, Eugene. Angry with myself for being a coward and running away. I've been an independent woman for quite some time, Eugene. My husband died almost fifteen years ago. I thought I'd collapse into pieces. Yet, I've managed to get along all right on my own since then. It hasn't always been easy. Certainly not at first. But, I'm a survivor, don't you see? I've made a nice life for myself here in Margate since then. I got to thinking while I was waiting for the bus and then I got angry. *(with conviction)* Nobody's going to run me out of Margate. Not the neighbors and their pitiful stares and whispers. And, certainly, not some witch in 204!

HERMAN. *(clapping)* 'Atta girl!

THELMA. You should have called me on my cell phone, Sylvie. I would have driven right over to get you.

(They all look at **THELMA** *like "you've got to be kidding".)*

THELMA. Never mind.

FANNIE. But, Sylvie! The witch – her name is Jezebella by the way. She's dangerous!

HERMAN. Fannie, come on. Let's go. I think Sylvie and Eugene need some time alone together.

THELMA. That's a good idea, Herman. Come on, Fannie. Let's leave these two alone to sort things out.

FANNIE. Sylvie, call me if you need me. And, I know why you came back and everything – but – I wouldn't go walking around outside quite yet if I were you. It's not safe.

SYLVIE. I appreciate your concern, I really do. But, I refuse to be a prisoner in my own apartment!

THELMA. Sylvie, Fannie's right. You must listen to reason.

SYLVIE. But...

FANNIE. *(suddenly overcome with glee)* Sylvie! I almost forgot! I have *Information!*

SYLVIE. You do? About what?

FANNIE. Now, I'm not saying this to make you feel bad. I know with what happened today the timing is probably not right to tell you, but...you'll never guess!

SYLVIE. What, Fannie? What is it?

FANNIE. Herman asked me to marry him! I'm engaged! *(she does a happy dance)*

SYLVIE. Mazel tov! Fannie, that's wonderful. I'm so happy for you.

(She hugs **FANNIE.***)*

Congratulations, Herman.

(She hugs **HERMAN.***)*

HERMAN. Thank you, Sylvie.

SYLVIE. Did you set a date? Have you thought about where you'll...

(There is a knock on the door and everyone freezes.)

THELMA. What should we do? It might be her!

FANNIE. Look out the peephole!

SYLVIE. Eugene! Quick! Hide in the bedroom!

*(***EUGENE*** hastily retreats to the bedroom taking* **SYLVIE***'s suitcase with him.)*

THELMA. *(goes to the door and bangs into in her quest to locate the peephole)* Holy crow! I don't believe it!

(THELMA opens the door.)

FANNIE. What are you doing! Are you crazy? Don't let her in!

(MABEL and EVELYN enter. EVELYN looks like she was run over by a truck can barely walk and is mad as a hornet. Now relatively sober, she delivers her lines ranting and raving.)

THELMA. Evelyn! What are you doing here!

(All rush to EVELYN's side and help her to the sofa.)

FANNIE. Evelyn, shouldn't you still be at the hospital?

HERMAN. How are you feeling?

EVELYN. I need a drink!

SYLVIE. I'll get you some water. *(She goes into kitchen and gets a glass of water.)*

EVELYN. I don't need water! I need a drink!

FANNIE. Evelyn, after everything that you've just been through, I don't think…

EVELYN. Where is *she*? Where is that crazy witch? Let me at her. I'll kill her. I'll wrap her shawl around her scrawny neck. I'll rip her eyes right out of her…

THELMA. Calm down, Evelyn.

EVELYN. Don't you "Calm down Evelyn" me!

THELMA. Okay, okay. *(to MABEL)* I can't believe they released her. Weren't they going to keep her overnight?

MABEL. She checked herself out.

THELMA. Evelyn, no! You should really be in the hospital. Please, let me drive you back.

(MABEL shoots THELMA a look as if to say that EVELYN's been through enough trauma for one day.)

THELMA. *(disgusted)* Never mind.

EVELYN. They think I'm crazy.

FANNIE. Crazy? Why?

EVELYN. Yeah. Crazy. *(points to MABEL)* And, it's all *her* fault!

SYLVIE. *(to MABEL)* What's she talking about?

EVELYN. *(finally realizing that* **SYLVIE** *is present)* Sylvie! You're here! You didn't jump off the control tower after all.

SYLVIE. Yes, I'm here, Evelyn. Now, please. Here, drink some water.

EVELYN. I don't want water! They pumped me full of water at the hospital. Do you have any nice white wine? Maybe some zinfandel? I'm afraid that red will bring back my headache.

SYLVIE. How about a diet Coke?

HERMAN. *(having drunk the last of it)* Er... All gone.

EVELYN. The Witch! She thought I was you, Sylvie! The Witch in 204! And, *they* wouldn't believe me!

SYLVIE. Who wouldn't believe you? The doctors?

EVELYN. *(frantic)* The doctors! The nurses! The lawyer who gave me his business card in the Emergency Room None of them would believe me! They all think I'm crazy. They all think I'm a nut case! They all think that I tried to kill myself. But I told them, "No! I didn't try to kill myself! *The Witch in 204* tried to kill me! *The Witch in 204* forced me to drink a poison brew that she kept in a secret pocket in her witch's cape – that's where she kept her private stash of poison potion." *None* of them would believe me! *(growling and pointing to* **MABEL***)* And *SHE* wouldn't stick up for me!

MABEL. Now, Evelyn...

EVELYN. Don't you "now Evelyn" me! You were going to let them lock me up! *(pleading to* **SYLVIE***)* I'm *not* crazy! I'm telling you, there is a *witch* living in 204 and she tried to *kill* me! Right here! Right in your apartment, Sylvie! And, she thought I was *you!*

FANNIE. *(sincerely)* We believe you, Evelyn.

EVELYN. Oh, you're just saying that! You don't believe me. Nobody believes me! And *her! (points an angry finger to* **MABEL***)* *She* just stood there letting them think I was crazy and suicidal. She even suggested that a few days locked in a padded room in the psych ward may do me some good.

MABEL. Evelyn, please. I didn't mention anything about a padded room. I just thought that...

EVELYN. And, do you want to know *why* she thought I needed a vacation in the Land of Thorazine? Do you want to know? I'll tell you! Because the handsome young psychiatrist who came in to examine me *wasn't wearing a wedding ring*, that's why! And when the nurse came in and said "Doctor, your ex wife is on line 2" Mabel's ears perked up and her eyes got wide like saucers and I could just see the wheels spinning round and round in that yenta brain of hers. And, when the handsome young divorced shrink came back into the room Mabel was all in his ear about how I may benefit from a few days R and R with the other loonies on the 5th floor – where he could personally keep an eye on me, being, you know, "suicidal" and everything. And, of course, she'd come to visit me every day and check in with him on my progress. Because she's such a good *friend* of mine! *(to MABEL, disgusted)* As if I don't know Bonnie's wedding is off and you're scouting around for a new suitor for her! You can't fool me, Mabel Millstein! Some friend! Ha!

SYLVIE. Evelyn, we *do* believe you about the witch. And, we've *very* relieved to know that you're going to be all right. We just think you should take it easy.

(EUGENE comes out of the bedroom.)

EVELYN. *(points and growls at EUGENE)* Yooooouuuuuuuuuou! The witch tried to kill me because of *yooooooouuuuuuuuu!* You're some kind of a *genie* and the witch was trying to talk to you in a *teapot!* *(to SYLVIE)* I told the doctors this but they wouldn't believe me! I don't know what's going on here, Sylvie! But, you ought to know the truth about your gentleman friend here. He's some kind of a genie and his ex-girlfriend is a wicked witch. *(to everyone and nobody in particular)* You know, they ought to fire the building management. The new resident screening process has gone to hell in a hand basket.

THELMA AND FANNIE. *(concurrently)*
    A genie? / Eugene, you're a GENIE?

SYLVIE. *(sits down)* Oh brother. I knew this was bound to happen eventually.

MABEL. Wait a minute. He's a genie? A *real* genie? *(to **SYLVIE**)* You *knew* this?

EVEYLN. And, his name is NOT Eugene! It's *(She struggles to remember.)* Genesis Ecuador Nicaragua something or other.

HERMAN. Is this true, Eugene?

EUGENE. It is true. I am a genie. However…

MABEL. You're a genie? A "three wishes" kind of genie? *(to **SYLVIE**)* No wonder you weren't interested the retired magician I introduced you to over at the senior center. You've got your own magic man. And, I bet he can do more than a couple card tricks.

EUGENE. As you know, Sylvie and I met last year when she spent a few days in Egypt. To the extent that you require more of an explanation I will be happy to accommodate at the appropriate time. For now, however, I believe we have more pressing matters than genealogy and sociology.

THELMA. I think I may just join you with that drink, Evelyn. I mean, first we learn there's a witch living in the building. And, now a genie? What's next? A warlock? A werewolf? I hate to say this, Fannie, but we should probably start thinking about moving. The value of our apartments is sure to drop the way this building is changing.

EUGENE. Please, before you all run off to nail "For Sale" signs on your front doors, I believe we all have a matter of common interest in need of our attention.

HERMAN. That being?

EUGENE. To rid ourselves of Jezebella. Now known as the Witch in 204. Mrs. Greenbaum, I have an idea. And, if you are feeling up to it, you may very well be of vital assistance.

EVELYN. Just give me five minutes alone with that witch! It's my turn to show her who's wicked! *(She imitates* **BELLA***'s cackle.)*

EUGENE. Spendid! That's the spirit.

SYLVIE. Eugene, what are you thinking? Hasn't Evelyn been through enough of an ordeal? I don't want her put in harm's way.

EUGENE. I will personally guarantee Mrs. Greenbaum's safety. With the assistance of our friends, if they will agree to cooperate, I am reasonably confident that we shall be able to protect her. And, protect you, Sylvie once and for all. Then, we can be married if you will still have me. *(looks around)* That is, if you are all in agreement?

MABEL. Well, I don't know.

EVELYN. You owe me Mabel Millstein! You let them think I was crazy!

MABEL. Oh all right. I'm in.

FANNIE. Me too!

HERMAN. I served in the Marine Corps! *(He salutes.)* Semper Fi! I'm not afraid of any witch!

EUGENE. Very well. In that case, we've got ourselves a witch to whack! *(He extends his arm forward with his hand palm down and proclaims:)* Whack the Witch!

SYLVIE. *(extending her arm, she places her hand on top of* **EUGENE***'s and proclaims:)* Whack the witch!

*(*FANNIE, HERMAN, MABEL, EVELYN *and* THELMA *all repeat the gesture, one at a time but quickly, by placing their hands on top of the last hand and,* **with courage and conviction**, *each of them individually repeat the mantra "Whack the Witch!" Then, in unison, they all recite a final "Whack the Witch" after which they raise both arms in anticipated Victory, as the lights fade quickly to black.)*

(Blackout/Curtain)

Scene Two

(Setting: The same, the following morning)

(At Rise: SYLVIE *and* EUGENE *are alone in* SYLVIE*'s living room going over the plan.* EUGENE *is dressed as a "genie" with harem pants, a vest, bare feet or moccasins, and a turban style hat with a broach and colorful feather. He is adorned with assorted jewelry and an earring.)*

SYLVIE. Eugene, I'm frightened. What if our plan doesn't work? Mabel was right. This is too dangerous.

EUGENE. *(embraces* SYLVIE*)* I admit, Sylvie, I am not entirely overconfident. However, I do have faith in our friends. And, should Jezebella be the witch that I remember her to be, if our plan works, we have an excellent chance of ridding ourselves of her once and for all. Surely by now she has realized I haven't locked myself away in that dreadful teapot and she'll come back looking for me.

SYLVIE. That's what I'm afraid of!

EUGENE. But, with Themla as our lookout, if things don't go as planned, she'll give a signal and we can call it off.

(There is a knock on the door.)

SYLVIE. That might be her!

EUGENE. *(peeks out peephole)* It's Herman. *(He checks his watch.)* Right on schedule.

*(*EUGENE *opens the door and* HERMAN *enters.)*

HERMAN. *(*HERMAN *enters in Marine Corps camoflauge jacket and field hat carrying a Bloomingdales shopping bag in his left hand. He gives a* EUGENE *a confident and proud soldier's salute and greeting.)* Lieutenant Herman Hyman Hirshman reporting for duty, Sir! *(checking out* EUGENE*'s attire)* Hey, I remember that costume. You wore it to the senior social last year. What was the theme? Desert Oldies or something?

SYLVIE. *(correcting him)* Seniors of the Sahara.

HERMAN. That's right. Fun party! It's a good thing you hung on to that costume.

EUGENE. Are your munitions ready, solider?

HERMAN. *(holding up Bloomies bag)* Checked and ready, Sir! *(He checks his watch, then to* **SYLVIE:***)* Sylvie, I think it's time for you to go.

SYLVIE. So soon?

HERMAN. Mabel and Fannie are already sitting shiva. Or, at least pretending to.

SYLVIE. So, the witch knows?

HERMAN. She sure does. Thelma tipped the newspaper delivery boy five dollars to slide a Shiva Notice under the door of 204 addressed to "Sylvia's Friends at Jerome Gardens." Thelma watched as the boy slid the notice under the door then knock and run away. She said the witch opened the door, read the notice and gave a horrible cackle. So, the witch thinks she killed you and made it look like suicide. *(to* **EUGENE***)* Oh, before I forget, Thelma said she can only stand guard in the stairwell for another half an hour. She's got a dentist appointment.

EUGENE. Well, it seems that our plan is underway.

SYLVIE. So, you think Jezebella will actually go upstairs to pay respects to Mabel and Fannie while they sit shiva for me?

EUGENE. Yes, because Thelma also put my name on the Shiva Notice along with Fannie's and Mabel's, with calling times. Jezebella will think that I am sitting shiva with them. And, I'm the one she's really after. Besides, what is the saying…"curiosity killed the cat?" Bella won't be able to resist paying her respects. She may even muster up an artificial tear or two in your honor. Just to make it look good.

SYLVIE. My goodness. She is heartless.

EUGENE. She certainly is.

HERMAN. Then when the witch asks where Eugene is, they'll tell her that he went to get something in your apartment.

EUGENE. Right. Jezebella will no doubt make a hasty retreat to come down here to find me.

SYLVIE. And who am I supposed to be?

EUGENE. A Shiva caller paying your respects to Sylvie's closest friends. It might look suspicious if Jezebella is the only one to stop by to pay respects. You can say you got a notice under your door too and were shocked to hear that Sylvie has passed. To make it look more believable.

SYLVIE. What if someone else shows up at Mabel's, like Rhoda Bennet or Sam Waterman? What if they see me? They'll know that I'm not dead.

HERMAN. We only prepared one Shiva Notice and Thelma watched the newsboy slide it under 204. She's standing guard in the stairwell and will intercept anybody else who may happen to try to knock on Mabel's door besides you and the witch. So, unless Mabel's pipes should burst and the maintenance man comes, or the building catches fire, you're safe.

SYLVIE. *(to EUGENE)* You've thought of everything then.

EUGENE. With Herman's help in tactical military planning. Good job, soldier!

HERMAN. *(salutes)* Sir! Good luck, Sylvie!

SYLVIE. You too, Heman.

> *(HERMAN retreats to his position in the bathroom and gets changed for witch combat.)*

SYLVIE. Oh, Eugene. This all sounds too risky to me. What if Evelyn gets hurt?

EUGENE. I won't let that happen. But, if you are apprehensive, there is always Plan B.

SYLVIE. What's Plan B?

EUGENE. I go off with Jezebella and spend the rest of my years in misery.

SYLVIE. Let's stick with Plan A.

EUGENE. Then, as the saying goes… It's show time!

*(**SYLVIE** gives **EUGENE** a quick kiss and exits.)*

EUGENE. *(knocking on bedroom door)* How are you coming along in there, Evelyn?

EVELYN. *(**EVELYN**, dressed in a white sheath with a white veil and white slippers wears white translucent makeup and bright red lips "floats" out of the bedroom and across the stage with arms extended and speaks in a ghost-like quivering voice.)* Boooooooooooo!!!!!!!!! I haven't had this much fun in years! Revenge is SO sweet! *(She twirls.)*

EUGENE. So they say. So they say. *(He goes to bathroom and knocks on door.)* Almost ready, Herman?

HERMAN. *(from bathroom)* Dressed and ready for combat, Sir!

EUGENE. Be patient, Soldier. The battle is just beginning.

(The phone rings twice then stops.)

HERMAN. *(enters from bathroom dressed like a Wizard and carrying a towel and a hairdryer)* That's Thelma's signal!

EUGENE. All right, you two. Prepare for battle stations. The witch must be on her way down.

*(**EVELYN** "floats" back to the bedroom.) **EUGENE** unlocks the front door to **SYLVIE**'s apartment and leaves it open a few inches. He then lies down in the on the living room sofa and covers himself from head to toe with a blanket. He then groans – **BELLA**'s cue to enter.)*

BELLA. *(entering, not noticing **EUGENE** on sofa)* Genesis Elijia! I *know* you're in here. It's no use to try to hide from me any long… *(She hears **EUGENE** groan on the sofa.)* Oh good! There you are. Resting up for our journey back to the homeland, I see. *(She peels back the blanket.)* It's so nice to see that you are finally dressed appropriately! Get up, sleepyhead. It's time to go.

*(**EUGENE** moans and clutches his chest.)*

Genesis! What is it! What's wrong! *(She rushes to him, and kneels along side him.)* What is it my darling? Are you ill? You are so very fortunate I arrived when I did, my sweet. *(She reaches into her handbag and pulls out a flask and holds it to his lips.)* Here, drink this. Let Bella make it all better.

*(**EUGENE** coughs and spits out the potion.)*

EUGENE. It is too late, Jezebella. I'm dying. *(He clutches his chest.)* My heart! My heart!

BELLA. Oh fiddlesticks. Genies don't have heart attacks. Your ancestry is immune from heart disease. Any wizard worth his salt knows this. The only way that anything could possibly be wrong with your heart is if...is if... *(She stops to think.)...* No! That's impossible!

EUGENE. You are wrong, wicked witch. It is indeed possible. In fact, verily I say unto you, it is quite true.

BELLA. But...but...how? No! I refuse to believe it! Get up! Get up this instant! We are leaving this horrid little town of Margate, New Jersey immediately. The beach is much to crowded. The ocean is entirely too chilly for this time of year. And, the people here are dreadfully boring. *(beat)* I must say though, the boardwalk pizza isn't half bad.

EUGENE. You will have to go on without me. I am soon to be a part of the other world. I wish I could say it was good to see you again, Bella. But, I can not.

BELLA. And why is that? Because I interrupted your folly of a plan to wed a commoner by the name of Sylvia Goldberg? You and I, Genesis...you and I belong together, and it is together that we shall be at last. I never understood why you have always had such a difficult time coming to terms with *The Arrangement,* my sweet. You must trust that the *Powers That Be* knew what they were doing when they *Arranged* our destiny. "What the Powers have *Arranged,* let no one put Asunder." Isn't that how the proverb goes?

EUGENE. Jezebella, even if I were in agreement with *The Arrangement,* which, as you well know, I am not, I will never agree to such an *Arrangement* whereby my destiny is shared with you! How many times and in how many different languages do I need to tell you that before *you* accept it?

BELLA. Because I'm a *witch?*

EUGENE. No. Because you are *wicked.* Always have been. Always will be.

BELLA. So? What's the fun of being a witch if one can't raise a little cain now and again?

(**EUGENE** *moans and holds his chest.*)

EUGENE. It's time, Jezebella. I bid you farewell.

BELLA. Not so fast! Who did this to you?

EUGENE. My one true love. Sylvia Goldberg. She is the one who broke my heart, thanks to you.

BELLA. No! To do that she'd have to have come back as a... as a... Are you saying, she's a...she's...here? Where? Where is she? (**BELLA** *looks around.*)

(**EVELYN**, *dressed as the ghost of* **SYLVIE**, *"floats in" from the bedroom carrying a large flash light turned on and sneaks up behind* **BELLA** *and startles her.*)

EVELYN. *(in a ghost-like quivering voice)* I'm right here, Jezebella! You poor pathetic excuse of a wicked witch. What's wrong? Your powers slipping away? Couldn't you feel my *presence?*

BELLA. *(startled and jumpy)* It's you! No! Impossible! You *can't* be a...

EVELYN. Ghost? Spirit? Apparition of death? Sticks and stones, Jezebella. You can call me whatever you want. Just don't call me late for *cocktails!*

BELLA. I don't understand? *(She paces back and forth, agitated.)* I *know* the *Rules!* In order to successfully paranormally return to haunt the halls of a former residence and claim real and personal property that belonged to you in the living world, you would need the assistance of a *(She looks around.)* you'd need the assistance *of a... Who* did this to you?

EVELYN. After what you did to me, you think I owe you an explanation? *(to* **EUGENE***, taking his hand and shining the flashlight into his face)* Come along, Eugene. *(She motions to the flashlight.)* The Light awaits us. It's time we walk together into the great ever after. *(She shines the flashlight into his face then hers.)*

BELLA. Stop! No! You leave him right where he is! He's mine. You can't have him.

EVELYN. Oh, it's too late for that, Bella. Eugene's heart broke when he learned that I expired at the hospital. All I had to do was scare him into a real heart attack when he saw me come back for him as a ghost. *(She snaps her fingers.)* Piece of cake! Now, thanks to you, Eugene and I will be together for all eternity.

BELLA. But, only the *Chosen Ones* get to come back! How did *you*, of all people, luck out? Who was your *Advocate?*

*(***HERMAN*** enters from bathroom dressed as a Wizard, in a black robe with a black hat on top of a long gray wig. He's got a long gray beard.* **HERMAN** *points a cordless hairdryer at* **BELLA***, as if it were a semi-automatic weapon, the handle of which is concealed by a colorful hand towel.)*

HERMAN. *(forcefully)* Be gone, Witch! There is no room for you here! Let the lovers get on their way.

BELLA. *(Incredulous, eyeing* **HERMAN** *up and down)* Who the hell are **you**?

HERMAN. You don't *remember* me?

BELLA. *(She studies him closely then, in disbelief:)* MERLIN???? Merlin, is it *really* you? After all these *years?*

HERMAN. Now, what is all this hogwash about an *Arrangement?* You know full well that I put the kibosh on any *Arrangement* involving the likes of you long ago. You proved to be *unworthy* of the *Arrangement.* Dare I remind you how?

BELLA. Oh, Merlin, that's *ancient* history. There's no need to dredge up old…

HERMAN. Let us set it straight for the record, shall we? Once and for all?

BELLA. *(embarrassed)* No, I don't think that's necessary at this point. After, all, you know I spent years in atonement and...

HERMAN. Remember the spell you cast, Jezebella? On the wrong subject? *(chuckling to* **EVELYN***)* You'll never guess who she mistook for...

BELLA. Oh Merlin! Why must you insist on embarrassing me like this! I was just a young witch! Must I continue to pay for one lousy mistake for the rest of my life?

HERMAN. *(laughing)* Some witch! Instead of turning a handsome young Prince into a horny toad she turned a horny toad into a...

BELLA. Stop already!

HERMAN. *(chuckling)* What's wrong, Jezebella? Is your pride hurt?

BELLA. I just don't believe it is warranted to bring up such trivial events from the past.

HERMAN. Well, you blew it then and there. Your utter carelessness proved to the *Powers That Be*, including myself, that any *Arrangement* made involving you were to be null and void. Now, as I was saying, *Be Gone Witch!*

EVELYN. Yeah! Be Gone Witch! Or else!

BELLA. *(snidely to* **EVELYN***)* Or else *what?*

HERMAN. Oh! You want to *test* me? *(He walks toward* **BELLA** *pointing the hairdryer.)* You want to test *my* power against *yours?* That is a pretty foolish thing to do, witch, but I'm game if you are. I *know* what I'm capable of. After all, look what I just did. *(He gestures to* **EVELYN***.)* She was dead as a doornail. Now she's one of the *walking* dead. Let's face it. If your powers were all what they are cracked up to be you wouldn't have to resort to modern day pharmaceuticals to supplement your witchcraft. If word gets out that you've been cheating with mother's little helpers your reputation, or, the little that's left of it, that is, is garbage. *(He holds up*

the hairdryer, still under the towel and points it directly at
BELLA.*)*

BELLA. What's that? What are you doing?

HERMAN. *(comes at her)* Let's just find out, shall we.

BELLA. It's nothing! It's just a modern day apparatus for drying hair.

HERMAN. Oh really? Then, shall we see what happens when I turn on this switch and…

BELLA. No. No! Stop! Stop!

HERMAN. This is no ordinary hair drying apparatus, witch! The currents of ten thousand lightening strikes are contained in this mechanism. You know as well as I do that it only takes three thousand strikes to whack a witch dead. Let's see what ten thousand currents can do, shall we?

BELLA. Stay away from me with that thing!

HERMAN. Ready or not! Here I come!

(Mayhem ensues during the next few moments with **HERMAN** *chases* **BELLA** *around the stage pointing the hairdryer at her and with* **BELLA** *trying to duck and escape from the hairdryer all the while they are screaming at each other, during which time* **EVELYN** *and* **EUGENE** *are doing their thing with the flashlight into eternity.* **BELLA** *eventually runs into* **SYLVIE***'s bedroom and slams the door closed.)*

BELLA. *(calling from bedroom)* Goodbye forever, Genesis Elijia! You and your despicable ghost girlfriend can rot in… AAAGGHHHH!

*(***HERMAN*** runs into the bedroom and shortly thereafter runs back out.)*

HERMAN. Eugene! For Pete's Sake! Eugene! She jumped out the bedroom window! I didn't mean for her to do that! Oh no! What did I do? What did I do!

EUGENE. *(gets up from playing dead on sofa and runs into the bedroom)* She did what?

HERMAN. Oh, this is terrible! I just wanted to scare her away, not kill her!

EUGENE. Herman, it is okay. Calm down.

EVELYN. Way to go, Herman! You've got your first jumper under you belt. You make a very convincing wizard!

HERMAN. It's not okay! She jumped out the window for crying out loud! Eugene, call an ambulance. I'm going downstairs to see if she's still alive.

(**MABEL** *and* **FANNIE** *enter in a dither and talk in rapid fire succession.*)

FANNIE. What's all the screaming for? What's going on in here?

MABEL. We were waiting next door! Out on the balcony.

FANNIE. Did somebody just toss a black cat out of the window?

HERMAN. A black cat?

FANNIE. We were waiting on the balcony next door to try to hear what was happening in here when all of a sudden we see a black cat dive out of Sylvie's window.

EVELYN. Is it dead?

MABEL. No, it landed on its feet and ran away. Into the bushes over on Ventnor Avenue.

FANNIE. Where's the witch. Did she ever show up?

HERMAN. Yes, and I scared her away. She jumped out of the window.

MABEL. No she didn't. It was a black cat. I saw it with my own eyes.

EUGENE. Where is Sylvie?

MABEL. She's still upstairs in my apartment. She's fine.

EUGENE. Is Thelma with her?

FANNIE. No, Thelma had a dentist appointment.

EVELYN. (*checks her watch*) It's cocktail time! I'll get Sylvie. (**EVELYN** *exits.*)

HERMAN. I need a drink (*He sits down.*)

MABEL. So, I take it, the witch is history?

EUGENE. I certainly hope so! Herman, you are to be commended for a heroic show of bravery.

HERMAN. I need a drink!

FANNIE. *(to* **EUGENE***)* So, are you finally going to tell us now? What's all this witch and genie business?

MABEL. Yes, Eugene. You definitely owe us an explanation! Are you a real genie or not?

EUGENE. It is true. I am a genie. That is no secret. But, not the magic kind. Like in story book fables. Anyone can be a genie. You, and you and you if you so choose.

MABEL. What are you talking about?

EUGENE. *(clears his throat and proceeds with a less-than-convincing succession of tall tales about himself and Jezebella)* You see, I am a member of a grassroots organization called *Greener Environments Need Innovative Energy,* the acronym for which is GENIE. We plan to relocate our worldwide headquarters across the bridge in Brigantine due to the uniquely balanced ecosystem there.

MABEL. *(disappointed)* Oh for Pete's sake. You mean you're an *environmentalist?* Not a *real* genie?

EUGENE. *(laughing)* Though not magic, I am indeed a "real" genie. That is, we members of our organization refer to ourselves as "genies." We are always looking for new members to join our cause to preserve and protect the environment. So, you see, you too can become genies.

FANNIE. Of all things! Wait a minute though. Who is the witch? And, why…

EUGENE. Again, let me explain. It's a rather sad situation, really. Jezebella and I met when she was a lobbyist for the pharmaceutical industry. We should have been at odds with each other, professionally, that is. But, *The Powers That Be,* in her organization and mine, stuck up an *Arrangement* whereby our organizations would co-exist.

MABEL. Oh, please.

EUGENE. I came to learn that Jezebella suffered from mental instability which has grown progressively worse. I venture to guess she even possesses a degree of multiple personality disorder. Her colleagues in the pharma-lobby grew weary of her temperament and shied away from her. I did not. Sadly, Jezebella mistook my gestures of collegial friendship to be somewhat different than what I intended.

MABEL. What does that have to do with her being a witch?

EUGENE. I'm getting to that. Jezebella then left the pharmaceutical industry to head a chapter of an organization called *Women Innovating Therapeutic Curative Homeopathy,* the acronym for which is WITCH.

FANNIE. And, members of that group call themselves "witches?"

EUGENE. In fact, they do! And, Jezebella then assumed a secondary personality – and "alter ego" as it were, as a witch.

MABEL. I'm sorry, Eugene. This all sounds fishy to me.

EUGENE. You are correct. Jezebella's role in the organization WITCH was, as you put it, quite fishy. Instead of looking to progress homeopathic cures for diseases, Jezebella, often "cheated" and relied on pharmaceuticals, passing them off as homeopathetic. Believing she was a real witch, she thought she could get away with it. Until, that is, she got caught.

FANNIE. My head is spinning.

EUGENE. In short, Jezebella was dubbed a "wicked" WITCH and the homeopathic organization booted her out.

(**SYLVIE** *enters.*)

SYLVIE. Oh, Eugene! Is it really over?

EUGENE. Yes, I believe it is. Which means, we have a wedding to plan, if you'll still have me!

FANNIE. Let's make it a double ceremony! Is that okay with you, Herman?

HERMAN. I need a drink!

MABEL. *(to* **FANNIE** *and* **HERMAN***)* I think we all need a drink after today. Come on, let's get going. I swiped a bottle of the good stuff yesterday when the bartender had his back turned. These two need some time alone. And, I need some time to digest all this GENIE and WITCH baloney. *(to* **SYLVIE***)* Where's Evelyn?

SYLVIE. I left her in your apartment. She's watching *Southern Women of Fulton County.*

MABEL. *(horrified)* Ye Gad! What time is it? *(She checks her watch.)* We're missing it! Of all days! Luke Stormweather is marrying Ashley Lee Drake-MacDonald-Merriweather today!

FANNIE. I saw the previews! Sarah Beth Sturdivant-Sutton-Hollister- is three months pregnant with Luke's fourth child and she disguises herself as one of the caterers and corners Luke and convinces him not to...

(During the talk about the episode, **MABEL** *and* **FANNIE** *completely (and temporarily) forget about the witch and quickly exit to catch their favorite daytime drama with* **HERMAN** *close behind them.)*

HERMAN. *(just as excited, talking over* **FANNIE** *and ushering her out the door)* I told you to tape it! Why didn't you tape it? Hurry up, we're missing the wedding...

SYLVIE. *(after they leave)* So, I take it you explained to them about G.E.N.I.E and W.I.T.C.H.?

EUGENE. I did.

SYLVIE. Did they believe you?

EUGENE. I do not think so.

SYLVIE. I was afraid of that. Did Jezebella really change herself into a black cat? Evelyn said that Herman saw Jezebella jump out the window. But Mabel and Fannie saw a black cat jump out and run into the bushes. How did you explain that one?

EUGENE. I didn't. Fortunately, I seemed to have been saved, at least for the moment, by the *Southern Women of Fulton County.* But, I'll come up with something. I'm afraid that I'll probably be making up stories for some time to come. But, like all of the daytime dramas your friends watch, this episode, too, will pass.

SYLVIE. So, you don't think the witch will come back? Are you sure?

EUGENE. Whether she be a wicked witch or black cat – I think Herman scared Jezebella off for good. For now, let us just be glad that she is gone and we are together.

(He takes her hands.)

Sylvia, I have loved you since the day you freed me from the bondage of that horrible teapot. Will you marry me?

SYLVIE. Yes, of course I will, Eugene.

EUGENE. No, Sylvia. I mean truly marry me in a real official ceremony. Not just a commitment ceremony presided over by Mabel the yenta.

SYLVIE. But, Eugene. How *can* we? I mean, you *are* a genie. In order to have a real ceremony we would need to apply for a marriage license. You would have to get a blood test and show identification and...

EUGENE. We could go to Vegas.

SYLVIE. Vegas! Of course! No blood test required! But, what about I.D.?

EUGENE. For the right price, I don't suspect that identification will be that big of a problem? Do you?

SYLVIE. No, I guess not. But, let me make one thing clear right now.

EUGENE. What is it?

SYLVIE. I *refuse to be* married by an Elvis impersonator.

EUGENE. Certainly not!

*(There is a knock on the door. **SYLVIE** and **EUGENE** look at each other in horror as if to suggest, "Oh no! Not the witch again!" **SYLVIE** goes to the door and looks out the peephole. She then opens the door. **THELMA**, looking despondent, enters carrying a large cardboard box.)*

SYLVIE. Thelma, you're back from the dentist so soon?

THELMA. Uh, I never got there. I'm too upset.

SYLVIE. What happened? What's the matter? Come sit down.

THELMA. *(sits down on* **SYLVIE***'s sofa holding the box)* I pulled out of the parking lot and got half way to the Stop Sign on Ventnor Avenue when it ran right in front of my car! I didn't have time to stop!

SYLVIE. Oh Thelma! Not again!

THELMA. *(holds up the box)* I didn't have the heart to leave it in the middle of the road. Will you help me bury it?

SYLVIE. You ran over *another* dog?

THELMA. No. *(beat)* A black pussycat! *(She holds up the box.)*

*(***SYLVIE*** and* **EUGENE** *look at each other with mouths wide open in disbelief as the lights fade to black.)*

End of Play

PROPERTIES

Witch's Table Props:
Assorted prescription medicine bottles on Witch's table. (One of the
    prescription bottles must contain baking soda with cap off.)
Gold chalice filled three-quarters with vinegar
Large red apple
Bottle of Snapple
Bottle of Smirnoff Vodka

Sylvie's Apartment/Backstage Props
Sylvie's wedding dress (an age appropriate tea-length dress - not a
    blushing bride's white gown)
Box of tissues
Camera
Makeup mirror/makeup case containing nail file, tweezers, etc.
Note from Eugene to Sylvie
Note from Sylvie to Eugene
Note from Sylvie to Eugene (Bella's switched version)
Preset plate of cheese/crackers/grapes/snacks on kitchen table or
    counter
Cordless phone
Coat Rack with sweater
Tray of hors d'oeuvres for Mabel to carry in
Suitcase
Bucket and mop in kitchen for Fannie to carry in
Mini cocktail wienies
Cup of coffee for Fannie to give to Evelyn
Diet Coke for Herman
Clutch purse (for Evelyn) containing flask with booze
Bloomingdale's bag with a towel poking out of the top
Hairdryer
Flashlight
Colorful towel
Bloomingdales bag
Medium size box (empty, for dead cat/witch)
Teapot/genie container

SPECIAL COSTUMES

Wizard costume for Herman (Hat, cape, white wig, long white beard)

Ghost costume for Evelyn (White flowing dress, white face powder, white floral hair wreath with white ribbons)

Witch costume for Bella as per stage directions for Prequel

A chic colorful shawl/cape with a hidden inside pocket to conceal a small flask of pharmaceutically-enhanced witch's brew.

Genie costume for Eugene – colorful harem pants, vest, turban with feather and gemstones, etc.

SENIORS OF THE SAHARA
The "Prequel" to THE WITCH IN 204
by Barbara Pease Weber

Sylvia Goldberg, a respectable retired New Jersey school teacher, brings home more than just souvenirs upon returning from her grandson's wedding in Israel. Sylvie's troubles begin when she realizes that the old teapot she purchased at an outdoor market is actually a priceless relic containing a geriatric genie "Eugene" with a bad back and a penchant for vodka and V8. Keeping Eugene a secret from her three best friends, Mabel, Thelma and Fannie, proves to be nearly as difficult as protecting herself from Eugene's former master who follows Sylvie home and threatens her at knifepoint. Be careful what you wish for, Sylvie Goldberg! You never know, it might come true. *Seniors of the Sahara* is a magical romantic comedy for seniors and "juniors" of all ages.